The Legend of THE HIVE

The Legend of THE HIVE

Maria Owsianka

Illustrated by
Anna-Maria Szymańska

PAGODA BOOKS

Designer: Jacqui Apthorpe

ISBN 0 946 326 71 1

Originated by R.C.S. Reprographics, Torquay
Printed and bound in Great Britain by
BAS Printers Ltd, Over Wallop, Hampshire

Contents

Introduction

I have wished for a long time to enter a hive and see the life of the bees from the inside; but even if that were possible, I would still only be a visitor. THE LEGEND OF THE HIVE is an attempt to go further – to enter not only a hive, but the *mind* of a bee.

Bees have a store of knowledge on which they can draw whenever necessary, and a law which they obey and which guides their behaviour in all circumstances. This is usually dismissed by people as being "only instinct". Visualising this knowledge as something written into their nature, and because it operates fully only within a colony of bees, I have called it the Hive Legend, and presented the bees as if they knew that this is a higher law to which they can refer. In the story, they must learn it and pass it on to others. This is to underline the unity of the colony, and interdependence of individual bees within it. The store of knowledge is there, to be used when the need arises.

My heroine, Deborah, is not a human being in the shape of a bee. Indeed, because of the social nature of bees, her values are quite different from human ones. Individual good, if such a concept exists in the bee world at all, is always subjected to the good of the bee family. Whenever human beings have attempted to create such a society, however, it has been held together by fear, and has not led to happiness. But bee society works wonderfully well, and seems to be based on what, in human terms, we would call love.

Deborah is not afraid for herself: all her concern is for the colony. Like all bees, she is ready to use her sting in its defence, although she herself would die as a result. (She does not do it, fortunately, because that would cut the story short.) A colony, as well as an individual bee, is therefore in many respects like a single living organism. A bee can only live as part of the colony. Left alone, she would die.

Why, you may ask, does only one bee in my story have a name? And why Deborah? Firstly, I did not want Deborah to appear to know some bees better than others. There may have been as many as sixty thousand bees in her colony, all of them sisters and equally close. Secondly, there is no other name as suitable, except perhaps *Apis*. *Deborah* comes from the Hebrew word for "bee". In having this name, she remains an individual, yet at the same time she stands for all the bees in the hive.

What follows, then, is an account of a bee's life, as accurate as the present state of knowledge allows, such as perhaps she could give us if only we could find a way to communicate other than through the imagination.

M.O

CHAPTER ONE

A Journey of Discovery

I CANNOT SAY WHEN I FIRST BECAME AWARE OF THE LIFE AND movement outside my narrow cell. As the awareness grew, in spite of the warmth and comfort around me, I knew that I had to get out into the wider world. Only a thin capping of wax divided me from that movement of which I should now become a part; but first I had to bite my way through.

Making the opening was a laborious process. But at last the moment came when I could put my antennae through the hole which I had made into the space on the other side. I felt around. Living waves seemed to move over my head, occasionally touching me, and then passing on. Slowly, as I chewed away at the wax, the opening grew larger. My head now emerged. Then, after a little more effort, I caught the edge of the cell with my front feet, and heaved myself out.

My body was still very new. In spite of my six legs, I stood rather shakily on the uneven surface; and the first few steps which I managed to take were not a great success. Those warm, living waves were now moving around me in every direction; and though I felt a sense of purpose and unity in the movements, I was too young and weak to join in.

As I stood there uncertainly, those who brushed past me were strangely familiar and comforting. I was at one with this crowd: they were my sisters. The sound of their activity vibrated from the surface on which I stood and

Welcoming the newcomer

became even more pronounced when I again stretched out my antennae to feel around me, touching first one of the passing bees, then another. Suddenly one of them, instead of hurrying on, stopped and touched me in response.

I cannot describe the thrill of that first communication. As our antennae locked together for a moment, I knew for certain that I was no longer a lonely, rather lost, newly-emerged bee, but a member of a family.

"Welcome, Deborah, little girl" said this sister. "You must be hungry. I have food."

I unfolded my tongue for the first time and sucked up the drop of sweetness which she offered. As the energy-giving fluid flowed into my body, her antennae continued to touch my own.

"To build up your strength" she answered my unasked question. "There is no need to hurry. Look around you and see what is going on in the hive. You will be told what to do when the time comes."

I tottered off, a little less unsteadily, concentrating now on moving my feet. Lift first and third leg on the left, together with middle leg on the right. Move them forward; put them down. Then lift first and third leg on the right and middle leg on the left. With practice, it was becoming quite easy. You cannot fall if three feet are always firmly on the ground. The whole point is to maintain the rhythm and not to allow your feet to become entangled. I mastered this basic skill after a few moments, and it increased my self-confidence at once.

As instructed by my sister, I began looking or rather 'feeling' around. I had eyes, of course: as I was to learn later, five of them – two large, compound eyes and three small, simple eyes. But eyes are of no benefit in the dark. For indoor use, I had something far better: my antennae. With these, I was to find I could feel, hear, talk, smell and taste. But for the moment, I still had to sort out my sensations into a meaningful whole.

The taste of well-being

I was now walking fairly efficiently on the vertical surface of the comb; not honeycomb, strictly speaking, as this section did not contain honey but young bees – my younger sisters, not quite ready to be born – maturing inside sealed cells, exactly like the one which I had recently left. Soon I reached a cell from which a baby was just emerging. She had to do it all in her own time, just as I had done: that was the best way. I moved on, only to meet another youngster, trying out her legs for the first time. I touched her. Her fur was soft, more delicate than that of older bees. "I am only a little older than you, and rather hungry myself" I told her. "Someone will come along soon."

Aware of my hunger, I stretched out my proboscis to a passing bee, who stopped to feed me. Mixed with the sweetness of nectar, there was another taste, which told me that all was well with our family. As our antennae touched, I was filled with a sense of well-being and contentment.

Walking up the comb, I came to the end of the sealed brood cells. Here, a group of bees was cleaning and polishing empty cells, from which young bees had recently emerged. I wanted to join in, but first I felt I needed a rest. One of these cells would be just right. I crawled in, head first, and then settled down.

When I came out again, refreshed, I found the cells close by were already finished. I walked along the arc they formed and felt inside each of them until I reached one which still contained debris, and began to tug with my mandibles at the edges of the old skin sticking to the walls. The work was quite hard. I backed out of the confined space, and touched a passing sister, asking her for another drink of nectar. The feeling of well-being, experienced earlier, grew stronger. I now returned to my task, removing all the loose material from the cell and polishing the interior until its surface was quite smooth. Other bees nearby were also working on this section of comb; and one particularly conscientious bee felt inside all the cells in turn to check all was in order.

I set off along the comb, and again crossed an area where the cells were still sealed. Now and then, I could feel a slight movement under my feet, as a young bee reached out from a cell to make her first contact with the colony. Then, for the first time, I came to cells which were open, and contained

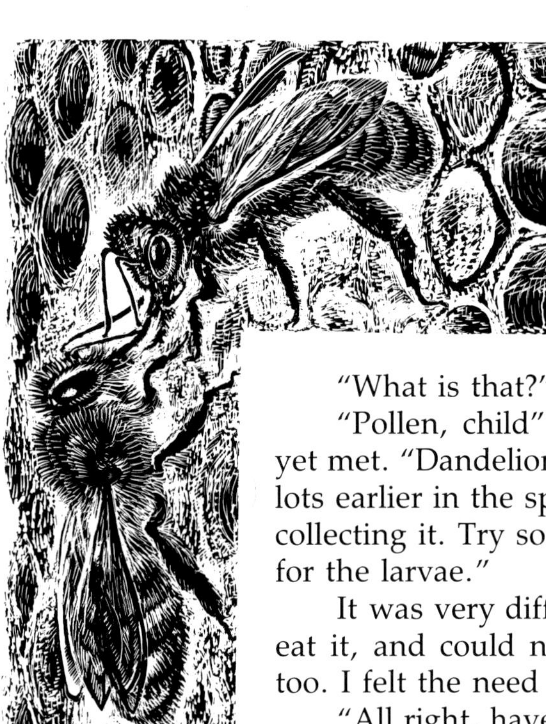

a powdery substance which I did not recognize. The atmosphere here was subtly different, and the bees crowding around had many different smells – not just the smell of the hive, but other strange aromas. I came across one bee who was half hidden in a cell, and I touched her protruding tail. She backed out and faced me, her head covered with the powdery substance, which she began to clean off.

"What is that?" I asked.

"Pollen, child" she replied. She was a much older bee than any I had yet met. "Dandelion pollen. The dandelions are nearly over now. There were lots earlier in the spring, but their pollen is still very good, and I am used to collecting it. Try some. You, too, will soon be eating pollen to produce milk for the larvae."

It was very different from nectar. I had to put it right into my mouth to eat it, and could not suck at it like a liquid. The taste-smell was stronger, too. I felt the need to wash it down, and stretched out my proboscis.

"All right, have some dandelion nectar. I have a little, and it goes rather well with the pollen" said the older bee, offering me a drink.

I could now feel the presence of many more bees: and as I was taking the nectar, I asked about the changes around us.

"It is evening" she answered "and rather cool. We are all coming back for the night. There are so many of us, it might be difficult to cluster. There's no longer enough room in the hive. But you, child, can stay right inside the cluster, as it's your first night. Keep warm."

She touched me once again, turned away, and disappeared inside the cell to finish packing the pollen which she had unloaded, pressing it down into the bottom of the cell with her head.

The last forager bees were coming in from outside, tired and cold, the fur on their bodies damp with dew. Some were pushing their way deep into the cluster to warm up quickly. There was constant, subdued chatter, the passing of news from one pair of antennae to another, and the exchange of food. Apparently, the weather had been good all day; but with clear skies, it became chilly at night. We huddled contentedly together.

Clustering together against the evening chill

"Each of us alone would be cold, but being in a cluster helps us to make our own heat. We can stay like this for a very long time, however cold it gets" explained the older bee next to me.

"Does it always get much colder at night?" I asked.

"Sometimes it does. But the real cold comes in winter."

"What is winter?"

"I am too young to know it from experience" she answered. "But the Hive Legend tells that it is a time of the year when days are short and nights long. For a lot of the winter, even the days are much too cold for bees to leave the hive. They must stay in a cluster to keep warm, living on the winter stores. Winter bees live very much longer than summer bees, but winter lasts so long that it spans the whole of their lifetime."

I wondered if winter was coming soon, but was told it was over, and that we would not live to see another. Now it was spring, and soon it would be summer. The night would not last long; and if the sun shone tomorrow, the foragers would be out shortly after sunrise.

The outside temperature fell further and the cluster around me grew closer to counteract that fall. Suddenly, I found that I was directly next to an open cell, the bottom of which was almost filled by something delicate and soft, curled into a ring, and gently pulsating with life. There was no need to ask anyone else what it was. In the same way that I had somehow known the other bees were my sisters, so I knew as I touched this creature that it was also one of us, only much younger, very vulnerable and in need of protection. In the coolness of early dawn, it had above all to be kept warm. I draped myself over the opening of the cell and shared my body heat with the baby.

A sister, only slightly older than myself, appeared and touched me. "Feeding time" she said. "I am making a round of all the babies in the area." As I moved aside, she inserted her head briefly into the cell and passed on. In the constant movement of the bees, someone else took over my post, keeping the baby warm, and I found myself drifting slowly and steadily towards the outside of the cluster.

Journeying up the comb

It must have been morning: the colony was stirring to life again. The cluster became looser, and certain foragers detached themselves from the rest, stretched their legs, refreshed their antennae by running them through the special brushes on their front legs, and rubbed their eyes. Then they set off downwards along the face of the comb. Meanwhile, we house bees had to close ranks quickly so that the brood in the centre would not get chilled.

The air outside warmed up after a time, and we became free to leave the brood in the care of the nurses and to wander off. During the night, I had been aware of deeper vibrations, different from those of the bees, and coming mainly from above; and I was now drawn upwards on a journey of discovery. The brood cells, full of babies at different stages, but progressively younger towards the top, came to an end: and there followed a band of open cells, containing something which I recognized.

It was pollen. I had tasted dandelion pollen before; but, here, there were many more types, each a little different. Some pollens consisted of tiny granules; others comprised particles that were bigger and more crunchy. In addition, as I was to discover later, the pollen paste was moistened with various types of honey, not necessarily from the same plants from which the pollen was derived. This created a variety that was almost endless.

The early foragers were already returning, and I was full of questions about this wonderful substance to which I felt myself strangely drawn. The pollen-gatherers knew, of course, the source of their harvest, and were ready to share their knowledge.

"This one comes from horse chestnut, which is a huge tree"I was told.

"Try this bluebell pollen, too" suggested another sister. "The bluebell is a small plant." I tried them, and liked both; but what was meant by a tree or by a small plant was a mystery to me. There was also pollen from hawthorn, holly, and many other sources.

"Pollen also has different colours" explained one bee. "Horse chestnut is brown, bluebell is blue-green, and hawthorn is pale green."

"What exactly are colours?" I asked, puzzled.

"You'll see when you go outside. Outside, you can see without touching, by using your eyes."

Meeting a stranger

I tried to imagine it, but gave up. It was too difficult. Instead, I tucked into the pollen, which had a delicious taste, and also made myself useful when an occasional bee found she could not get at some part of her body to clean it. The base of each wing, and the waist, between the thorax and the abdomen, were the most difficult places from which to remove pollen. I helped to brush it off, and added it to my diet.

All the while, the vibrations which I had set out to investigate were changing and becoming nearer, and I felt something bigger and far stronger than myself brush past me on the way down. Replete now with pollen, I continued my journey upwards, only to find that the pollen cells soon came to an end. What followed was honey, some of it capped, some in open cells and ready to hand. A small army of house bees was adding more nectar, freshly brought in from the field, and evaporating some of the water-content on their tongues to make it into honey.

But not only worker bees were present. Sitting there on the honey, I touched another large creature, just like the one which had brushed past me on the way down, and it responded to my touch with a deep vibration of its whole body. It was much bigger than a bee and more solid, yet it communicated gentleness. The huge head and furry body, meanwhile, exuded strength. In spite of this, it was also in an odd way helpless, and I began to feel protective towards it. When it asked for a drink, I shared out some of the nectar from my honeysac; and as our antennae touched, I knew who he was. He was my brother.

He appeared to want to move away, and I stopped him.

"Where are you going?" I asked.

"Outside" he answered. "We always wait until the sun is really hot."

"But field bees have been out since dawn" I protested.

"Yes, only because we drones stayed behind to keep the hive warm" he answered. "You, youngsters, could not do it by yourselves. You do not generate enough heat."

Other drones also began to move, and I followed them some of the way down. But I knew it was not the right time for me to go outside as yet. There were things to be done. From below came the throb of the drones' wings as they took off, the sound reverberating along the wooden walls of the hive.

It was now definitely time to look for work. I investigated other combs, searching out cells which needed cleaning, and either joined a group already at work, or was the first to discover a place where there was work that needed to be done.

Walking on the sealed brood cells, I occasionally came across one which appeared empty. On investigating, I found that it usually contained something which was once a larva, but which had died before maturing. What remained was a shrunk, sunken corpse. It had to be taken out and the cell cleaned. I knew that these few, premature deaths would not greatly affect the growth of the colony, if at all; nonetheless it was a sad duty to remove these little bodies.

As we continued the cleaning, older bees often passed us, carrying nectar to the storage above. They were always ready to give us food when asked. At last, the whole area of comb was finished, and my workmates drifted away in various directions.

Filled with the satisfaction of a job well done, I rested where I was, but not for long. A dense crowd of bees was coming towards our newly-cleaned comb. As they came closer, I sensed that something special was happening, and that it was an event of importance. Though eager to learn what it could

"So the feeling that all was right with our bee world had a source in our mother, the Queen."

be, I found it difficult to communicate since all the bees I touched appeared to be facing towards the centre of the group. At last one of them turned purposefully around and offered food. I took it, not knowing that it was anything special; but the feeling of well-being and harmony which accompanied the exchange was almost overwhelming.

"What is this?" I could not help asking with wonder.

"You have just had a share of the Queen substance" came the answer.

"There is enough to make everyone feel contented; but the nearer you are to the Queen, the greater share you have in this happiness."

So the feeling which I already knew and recognized, that all was right with our bee world, had a source in our mother, the Queen. I must indeed have been quite close to her, the happiness was so strong. I turned aside, seeking a sister with whom I could share what I had just found, and so that she, in turn, could pass this substance of happiness to others. Then I followed slowly the receding procession. Where the Queen had passed, there had been a change. Her scent now lingered on those cells which I had so recently polished; and when I felt inside, I found that each now contained an egg, standing upright on the bottom.

Savouring this feeling of completeness a little longer, I ambled towards the pollen combs for another meal. Something told me that this was also a duty; that the pollen which I was eating would benefit not only myself, but others as well.

I continued on and up, as far as the honey cells, where I came face to face with a drone who was busily cleaning his antennae, his huge eyes and his wings. I stopped by his side to tidy myself up, too, and he took the opportunity to ask me for help, which I gladly gave.

Then we shared some food. I gave him some of the Queen substance, although I did not know if it would mean as much to him as it did to me. His mind seemed to be elsewhere.

"The world looks beautiful from high up above the trees" he mused, as he took what I offered. We dozed off in companionable silence, sitting side by side on the honeycomb.

CHAPTER TWO

Finding my Wings

THE NIGHT-TIME ROUTINE OF CLUSTERING, WHEN THE HIVE seemed packed almost to the limit, soon became familiar to me; but the morning brought a change of mood and rise in activity.

I continued with my household duties, at the same time preparing for what lay ahead by feeding on pollen. Towards the warmest part of the day, however, I tried something new.

Instead of going up the comb to feed on pollen, I went down. Since pollen is stored all around the brood area, it does not much matter in which direction one looks for it, but going down had another result. I saw a faint light coming from under the combs. There was not much of it, but it was the first time that I had actually used my vision.

"You can see without touching, by using your eyes" an older bee had said. This, then, must be what she had in mind.

Below me was a flat surface across which several shapes were moving. I could see them, although they were much too far away for me to touch. Another bee brushed past me on her way down. I, too, walked downwards, right under the combs, getting as near to this flat surface as I could. I looked again. I could feel the bees around me; and, as they became visible in the light, I realised that the sister I had just touched became a strange, moving shape as she dropped down from the comb. So these strange shapes were other bees. I also dropped down, stood and looked. What I saw was a broad band of light, towards which my sisters were walking. I wondered at the novelty of being able to see so many things at once, but found that sight does not impart the intimate knowledge given by touch.

Seeking reassurance, I stretched out my antennae towards a bee who had just tumbled off the comb next to me, and was brushing herself down prior to going out of the hive. She responded to the contact, but in a slightly absent-minded way, since she was in a hurry to leave. I saw her move towards the light, open her wings and disappear. Silhouetted against the bright exit were other bees, coming and going, pausing at the threshold, taking off and landing. Most of those coming in found it easier not to walk up the combs, since these did not touch the floor and left a gap too big to reach across, too small for flying. It was easier to walk up the inner wall of the hive, thereby taking a less direct route.

I walked right up to the exit. It was not a very safe place. Field bees were coming in, heavily laden, and did not expect to meet a hesitant youngster just where they intended to land. Sometimes they managed to veer at the last moment, but even so I was the cause of several minor collisions. The landing field bees were not exactly angry, but too preoccupied to stop and exchange niceties. They picked themselves up, and hurried inside.

At last I found a place on the side of the exit, opposite the main landing area, where I was not in the way. I stood and looked, rubbing my eyes. The outside world had a depth and a variety of shapes which I had not suspected. I noticed a few tiny objects standing out against the uniform background. Perhaps these were the big trees and small plants, all of which gave pollen and nectar. A sister landed and inserted her proboscis into the very centre of one of them. It was a tight fit. The bee was big and heavy in comparison, and the whole structure swayed under her weight. A returning worker gave me its name.

"That's a flower" she said. "A forget-me-not."

I remembered my question of the previous day.

"Does it have a colour?" I asked.

"Yes. Blue. Like the sky. That is why we can see them so vividly."

"My sister indicated the huge space overhead, filled with an expanse of light. One thing was so big, the other so small, but what they had in common was their colour."

Our first flight

My sister indicated the huge space overhead, filled with an expanse of light. One thing was so big, the other so small, but what they had in common was their colour.

"So this is colour" I thought.

I stood looking at the sky. From the distance, bees flew straight towards me, grew quickly larger, and landed. They folded their wings and ran in. If their baskets were overflowing with pollen, the movement was awkward: they waddled rather than ran.

A group of young bees, which I had not noticed before, was now standing at my side. I do not know what told us just then that it was time for our first flight. There was no one to issue instructions. Yet all of us knew that it was to be a short flight, and that we must not take our eyes off the hive entrance.

I opened my wings, which then hooked together, so that each fore and hind wing would work as one, and launched myself off the landing board. Others did the same. We turned immediately in the air, and began to fly from side to side, facing the hive. A picture was building up in our memory of the position of the hive entrance in relation to our surroundings. The sun was high up, almost directly to my left, but only patches of sunlight reached the hive, which was partly shaded by trees. The sky on the opposite side from the sun was a deep blue, even deeper than the forget-me-nots.

Our orientation flight lasted only a few minutes: and foragers returning home must have been taking special care, as not one accident occurred. There was quite a large crowd of us in the air now, going through the same rhythmical, swinging movements, and taking in every detail of our surroundings, every angle.

Feeding the brood

Landing on the alighting board, I did not stall sufficiently and came down with a bump, but picked myself up and marched in. In darkness, on the familiar comb, among the densely packed throng of my sisters, I asked one of them in the old way, by touch, for food.

"I have just been outside for the first time" I told her, as our antennae touched. She understood all that this contact was meant to convey. From that day, I would be a creature of two worlds: the dark comfort of the hive, and the brilliant, perhaps dangerous, world outside. Life held more variety than I could ever have imagined.

☆ ☆ ☆

As I walked about during the latter part of the day, lending a hand here and there, various changes seemed to be taking place within my body. A pressure was building up inside my head: a sense of fulness and a need to share. I was drawn towards the open brood, especially those older larvae, lying curled nose-to-tail in their cells, whose only aim in life so far had been to eat in order to grow big and strong before their metamorphosis could begin. When I touched one of them, it responded with a slight movement and with an aura of expectancy.

I stroked the soft, supple body with my antennae, sensing its need for food. It moved forward a little, revolving in its round cradle. I opened my mandibles and placed a tiny drop of milk just in front of the baby's head. It moved forward and took the liquid. Full, it then became motionless again, and relaxed. I passed on to the next cell, where a fat occupant was equally ready for the milk.

Encountering queen cells

As the feeding progessed from cell to cell, the tension in my body began to decrease. If I strayed too far in my round and, instead of a plump, circular baby filling the bottom of the cell, came across a minute, newly-born larva, floating in its private pool of milk, I touched it and passed on. It was being cared for by older nurses. I felt comfortable and happy, the tension now gone. I had discovered what my next task was to be. It made me desperately hungry, however, and sent me in search of more food.

Next morning, the older nurses signalled that important events were about to take place in the colony. A feeling of expectation and subdued excitement spread around, and many bees began to gravitate towards the lower part of the brood area on the two inner combs. Several of us were already gathered round; and after a while, the news spread from one pair of antennae to another.

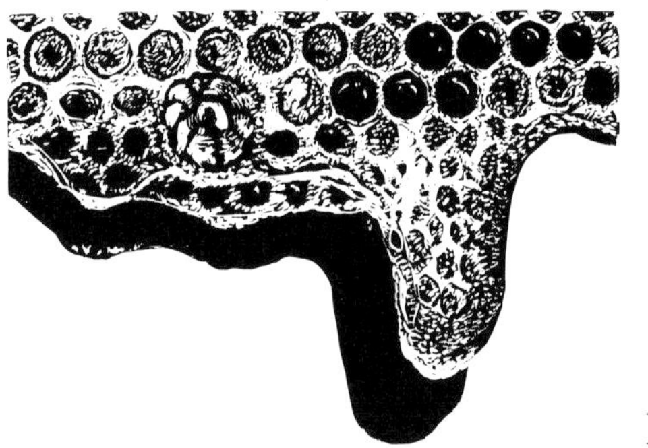

"The royal eggs have begun to hatch!"

I worked my way slowly into the centre, and saw that attention was focussed on a few cells that were quite different from the rest. Instead of being built into the comb almost horizontally, they were hanging vertically under a portion of comb cut short for the purpose. They were also much bigger, and each had a space to itself. They had rounded rather than hexagonal walls, and a rough outer surface. Some bees were busy on the edge of the downward opening, adding more wax and elongating the structure still further. I did not look right into the cells, as I did not feel that I was entitled to interfere with the care of the special larvae they contained. By the number of nurses that looked in to deposit their milk, however, I imagined the little princesses must have been floating in a veritable lake of food.

The weather continued to be fine and warm. That afternoon, I went for my second observation flight, and progressed to circling above the roof of the hive, looking at it from every direction. As long as I kept the hive in sight, I knew that I would be able to return to it with confidence.

Re-entering the hive, I noticed two or three bees lying motionless on the floor. I touched them. They were no longer bees, but empty, lifeless shells. An older bee came up at that moment.

Older bees make way

"We have to take them out of the hive, to make room for the living" she said. "But you are too young for this work. If you could just help me to drag the bodies towards the exit, I will fly out with them myself."

We began to drag one of the bodies forward. It was quite heavy, and we were glad of the help of another young sister who was passing. We heaved it out on to the alighting board, but could never have flown out carrying the weight between us. Such co-ordination simply was not possible. Anyway, the older bee had said that I was still too young.

I watched her as, balancing carefully on her back legs, she picked up the dead bee with her four remaining legs and took off. I turned back. Another sister was beginning to drag out the other dead bee. I volunteered to help, but did not release my hold in time and so was dragged off the alighting board and into the air. I found myself entangled, and fell down into the grass, still attached to the dead bee. I extricated myself and looked around. Blades of grass were waving above my head and I could see the sky; but where I was, there was shadow. I would never be able to take off from such a place. I began to climb a blade of grass to find a better position. Near the top, another bee was clinging on, and I moved to the other side so that our feet touched and we could talk. It was an elderly bee, and she looked tired. I was not well supplied with food, but might still find enough to share. I offered her some.

"No, thank you" she answered with her antennae. "I am not going to eat any more."

"Aren't you hungry?" I asked with surprise.

"It does not matter. I came out to die."

"Why should you die?" I asked.

"Because I am old and tired, and no longer useful" she replied.

"But I am happy. My family is strong. The Queen is doing well, and will go out with a beautiful swarm as soon as a new princess has been reared to take over."

"The new princesses have been hatched today" I told her.

A mysterious, large white object

"Good. Then all is well. Every bee should know when her time has come to return to the Hive Spirit. I am glad that the sun is shining, and all is well. Go back to the hive. You still have a lot to contribute."

"But can't you fly back, too?" I inquired. "You would then die near to your sisters."

"And get in the way, and have another youngster like yourself take out my body? It's quite unnecessary. I am going to die here, facing the hive, and in the sun."

I touched her in tacit agreement. I was balanced precariously on top of the blade of grass, and now engaged my wings and revved up before letting go with my feet. It worked. I flew back home, leaving behind the old lady according to her wishes. I was ready, as she had said, to contribute as much as I was able.

☆ ☆ ☆

The following day, the fifth of my life, was spent wandering around the hive, looking for jobs that needed to be done, with my time divided between feeding the brood and cleaning. While busy in this way, I met many drones on their way down from the honey store, prior to leaving for a flight. Drones seemed to prefer being in two places: either right up under the ceiling on the honey, or out in the sun. At least in that way, they were less in the way of brood-rearing bees. I was tempted to follow them, and also flew out for a short while, only to meet with a surprise.

Something which I had never seen before appeared very close: a large, white shape, not as big as what I now knew to be trees. It was behind the hive at first and then appeared before the entrance, blocking my flight path. I landed on it and contemplated my next move.

Before I could take a decision, however, part of it, warm and alive, slid under my feet, invitingly, and I found myself walking on to it. As usual, I walked upwards. On reaching the summit, I looked around. Nothing else had changed, the hive looked just as it normally did, and I could easily fly back. I settled comfortably, wiped my eyes, repeatedly brushed my antennae, then took off in my own time and landed at the hive entrance. This very strange giant appeared to be gentle enough.

In the presence of the Queen

However, after a short while I was forced to review my opinion. The covering of the hive suddenly disappeared and unfamiliar sunlight flooded the top of the combs. The presence of this being was somehow connected with the event. To make matters worse, the faint but terrifying smell of smoke now reached my senses. Tribal memory, of mortal danger to the family, stretching back millions of years, flooded my consciousness. Smoke meant a presence of fire; and as the Hive Legend emphasizes, bees have very little chance of survival in a forest fire. The only hope, but a slender one, lies in filling up with honey and leaving the hive, on the chance of escaping the flames and setting up a colony elsewhere.

Some of the combs containing honey had been broken during the lifting of the crownboard. I rushed in to fill up with as much of the store as I could, attempting to save it from destruction. Then I moved quickly down the comb, trying to get away from the light. In the rush, I bumped into a group forming the court near the Queen.

Here, however, there was no sign of panic. Concentrating on their mother's activity, the bees remained calm and their very mood soothed my nervousness.

Inexplicably, at that moment, the comb was lifted out, and sunlight flooded the whole scene. It was then that I saw what I never expected to experience with my eyes, as it always takes place deep inside the hive. The Queen was walking sedately in my direction, stopped to inspect a cell, and inserted her abdomen to lay an egg.

The tremendous upheaval around her and the sudden blaze of light did not appear to disturb her in any way.

As she came very close, I touched her reverently, and that feeling of well-being, derived from a share of the Queen substance and already so familiar, now overwhelmed me as I licked her body. I could hardly bear it. The Queen substance had to be shared quickly, both for the sake of my sisters and for my own safety. There was too much of it for any one bee. The apparent destruction taking place in our hive had almost been forgotten.

Two princesses suffice

Once the comb had been returned, the hive resumed its comforting darkness. I tried to settle down and continue my usual duties, but found it difficult as our ordeal was not entirely over. Other combs were being taken out and put back again; but when the roof was finally replaced on the hive and a measure of normal life returned, I became aware of the near-panic of the royal nurses.

"The princesses!" they signalled. "The princesses have been taken away!"

This was disastrous news. There were far too many bees in the colony to allow for further expansion, and it had been decided days ago, even before I was born, that the time was ripe for swarming.

Special Queen cells had been built with loving care, many more in fact than were needed, since only one Queen had to be raised to replace our mother, who was to go out with the swarm. Eggs had been laid in the cells by the Queen, and this was where the attention of the community was concentrated. When, after three days, they hatched into larvae, they were given the best food and supreme care. Without a young princess to take over, the swarm would not be able to go out, and to start the whole process again would mean a delay of five days.

Were all our plans to be thwarted at this stage? Had there been some mistake, I wondered.

Joined by other young bees on the way, I went to see for myself. Where some of the Queen cells had been, there was now a large gap, the edge of it torn. Some of the royal jelly, still staining it in places, was being licked up by the nurses. Other bees, distraught, milled around, attempting to repair the damage, an impossible task.

I moved along the edge of the comb. All was not lost. One beautiful cell had been left quite intact. I turned to the attendants to make sure.

"All is in order here" they answered. "This one has not been damaged in any way."

They fussed lovingly around their charge. On the other comb, it was the same story. A single princess had been left, but the others taken away. A feeling of relief slowly spread throughout the colony.

"Two princesses will really do quite well" came the verdict.

"At that moment, the comb was lifted out, and sunlight flooded the whole scene."

Repairing the damage

Our ventilation system had been completely spoilt by the opening of the hive and the effect of the smoke, and we now set out to restore a current of air around the hive. I joined those bees who were fanning on one side of the floor, holding on firmly with my feet and beating my wings vigorously as if flying in one spot, drawing the air out. It was difficult to keep my balance. The V-formation of bees moved slowly forward, until those at the front gave up, while others were continuously joining at the back. All this activity was surprisingly tiring and none of us could keep it up for long. But soon the smell of smoke was almost gone.

Feeling that danger was now past, I went back to the honey store to replace the honey I had taken in panic. But the cells at the very top of the combs had been broken, and I had to find room elsewhere. There was now repair work to be done, broken-off pieces of wax to be carted away, and the frames containing combs to be fixed securely. For that, *propolis* (or bee glue) was necessary. This is normally collected from trees and plants which exude resin, but in an emergency we could re-use that which was already in places within the hive where it was perhaps less essential. We scraped it out with our mandibles, and used it to fill with care every crack created when the

hive interior had been pulled apart. I kneaded the substance until it was soft, placed it in the cracks and smoothed it down carefully, making an even surface. After a while, I left the others to carry on with this sticky job, and went back to nursing. Whatever else happened, I was aware that the brood must never be neglected.

The babies in my present round were slightly younger than before, and did not completely fill the bottom of their cells. They had already finished all the extra food with which a new larva is supplied in the beginning, and were being fed mouth-to-mouth. I popped my head into each cell in turn, checking the babies and leaving a drop of food before each hungry mouth. The amount of pollen I had to eat so that it could be changed into milk was quite enormous. This meant there was less and less time for anything other than feeding myself in order in turn to feed the babies. As far as other work was concerned, this now had to be left to other, younger bees.

The first sound of rain

The day finished earlier than usual. A sudden in-rush of foragers had been followed by a sound which I had not yet heard, but which turned out to be the drumming of rain on the roof of the hive. The air outside was cooler, and we formed our night-time cluster, as loosely as space would allow, since within it babies had to be tended, pollen and nectar unpacked, and the latter evaporated to the consistency of honey. I lent a wing with the process of evaporation, fanning vigorously in one spot, so that a stream of air passed over the freshly-gathered nectar. Since the air outside was also saturated with water, there was more effort involved in the honey-making than there had been on previous nights.

The morning, I was told, was misty and damp, as it had rained for most of the night. Even though it was quite late, there was no sign of our drones. They were all sitting comfortably upstairs, covering us with a warm, living quilt against loss of heat.

The hive was overcrowded. Very few bees had ventured out, and they now returned wet and miserable. Others, who had decided to stay, were

Nursing the royal princesses

crotchety and useless, getting in the way of house bees and nurses, and unwilling to help with the work that had to be done. The best way of handling this situation was to ignore them as far as possible. For me, this was easy. I was concentrating entirely on my nursing duties, feeding the very young brood. Field bees tended to keep away from nursery areas.

In the afternoon, the sun came out at last. At once, more room was apparent in the hive, which made the tasks of nursing and housework far easier. It was my turn to feed the newly-hatched larvae, by placing the milk carefully around them, which allowed them to take as much as they needed at any time. I was now producing very high-quality milk, the sort that is given to larvae in the first three days of life.

"Food fit for a Queen" I thought happily as I went about my duties.

It was indeed fit for a Queen – or, rather, for a Queen larva. When I found myself near the two remaining princesses, I now looked into their cells. They were progressing well. One was in her third day after hatching; the other, a little younger. I added some of my food to their store, although they would probably never finish all they were being given. Nothing, however, is too good for a prospective Queen, and now we had only two of them in our care. It was a privilege to be a royal nurse, even if it was to be for just a short time.

We clustered around their cells, keeping the princesses warm, and giving them our love. One of the two would take over the colony after the swarm left with the Queen. Our whole future depended on her well-being: so for the rest of the day, as I continued looking after the brood, I made frequent visits to check on royal progress and to give the best of my milk to the two Queen larvae.

The following day began as usual. After a round of duties and a feed, I thought I might stretch my wings outside, and perhaps fly a little farther. But soon I saw that there was something wrong. Quite a number of guard bees were present near the hive entrance. We usually put out only token guards, as there was no other colony of bees near us, and so little danger of being robbed by our own kind. This time, however, the guards were numerous and standing front legs raised, eyes and antennae at attention. They were not checking on incoming bees, but made quick, repeated dashes to the landing board outside.

Something strange was taking place. I stood beyond the long line of guards, not wanting to distract their attention by asking questions, and observed. Bees were landing, heavily laden, at the entrance, and there was a lot of movement. After a while, I saw a shadow move quickly across the hive entrance. Suddenly, one bee disappeared, just as she was running in. A few moments later, another seemed to vanish in exactly the same way, snatched before she had time to enter. I moved forward gingerly, and looked out.

"You may not be in danger, but be careful" signalled one of the guards. "This creature seems to prefer returning foragers. That way, it gets both the bee and the nectar."

There was another flutter outside; but this time, the enemy retreated without success. I could see now that it was a flying creature, very much bigger than a bee. It appeared to have only two legs and two wings, but both the wings and the body had the same, uniform covering. It landed away from the hive, but was still in sight.

"What is it? I asked one of the guards during the short respite.

"A bird" she answered. "It used to come close and watch us, but never dared to fly in among us until now. We may be in trouble once it has learned how to catch bees, but we cannot really stop it."

I could smell an angry scent around us, one that caused me to raise slightly the tip of my abdomen and loosen the sting in its sheath. It was an automatic reaction. The guard who was talking to me asked for food. I offered some, and she continued.

"Yes, we've tried stinging it. The scent of the venom still lingers. But so far it's been useless. There's nothing to sting on this creature. The layer of feathers on its body is much too thick for a sting to penetrate."

The bird made another dash, and again caught a bee. It must have learned that if it held the bee's head in its beak, she could not sting. The whole movement was very quick, and it flew off at once to what it judged to be a safe distance to feed.

"We must get more bees together, and crowd it out" decided the guard.

"It may be frightened by numbers. Thank you for the food."

She went deeper into the hive to engage her troops. At that moment, I saw a drone who had just passed me, pause to wipe his eyes.

It was to be a disastrous delay. As he was about to fly away, the bird's beak grabbed him.

I moved aside as more guards arrived. They were ready for action; and when the bird next attacked, it was met by a score of bees flying into its face. A few more attempts and it gave up, and took off. Some of the guard bees returned to the hive, but many more than usual stayed at the entrance. From now on, this would have to be watched constantly.

My free time, in which I had intended to take a flight, soon ran out. I went back to the babies, but felt uneasy about this new development. There were more dangers to bees than it had at first appeared.

Would that bird constitute a serious danger to our colony? To the Queen, perhaps?

When we clustered together during the night, I repeated these questions, seeking answers from an older bee. I could feel that I was not alone. Many others were worried, too. Since our family had no experience of birds, we would have to rely on the Hive Legend. Birds could be dangerous, it told. The Queen was safe, as she did not normally leave the hive except during swarming,when there would be so many bees around that no bird would be able to find her. On the other hand, when the new princess went out on her mating flight, there might be very real danger.

"The Hive Legend talks about birds which are even more dangerous" an older bee warned. "Woodpeckers, for example, could destroy a whole colony. They make a hole in the hive and take out the bees, one by one."

Other enemies were discussed; bears, for instance.

"What are bears?" I asked.

No one in our hive had ever seen a bear, and there was a feeling that bears had not been around for a long time. But, of course, they could always appear again.

"But what are they like?" insisted several younger bees. "Are they as big as a bird?"

It was only the bee-keeper

"Very, very much bigger. They are covered with dark fur, much longer and thicker fur than the fur of a bee. They don't catch adult bees, but will open the hive and eat the honey and our babies."

"It is lucky that we haven't seen one for a long time, but it's best to be on the look-out" we decided.

"If you see something big, dark and hairy near to the hive, take no chances. Sting!"

We considered the possibility of such a happening, and determined that we would do our best always to be on guard.

"Someone opened the hive two days ago. Perhaps that was a bear" suggested a bee.

"Don't be silly, dear" answered an old forager. "That was only the bee-keeper."

The young bee insisted on the possibility, but the suggestion was again rejected.

"The Hive Legend says that a bear will break up the hive and leave chaos. Our hive was put together again, although it must be admitted that the inside was disturbed a lot. But the creature was not dark and hairy. It was white and smooth. The Hive Legend also does not tell of any connection between bears and smoke. This creature is definitely connected with smoke. I remember seeing it before, earlier in the spring. That time, the hive was also pulled apart and put together again, and there was smoke all around."

"That was definitely not a bear. It was a bee-keeper" said another senior bee with an air of finality.

"Is the bee-keeper also part of the Hive Legend?" I asked. No. The bee-keeper was quite a new element as far as bees were concerned and not part of the Legend.

"Should it not be made a part of it?" pressed another youngster. The colony definitely disagreed.

"The Hive Legend has never been altered" said the older bees. "It is passed on faithfully from generation to generation, and could not take into account changes which may be temporary." No one knew the origins of the Hive Legend. Perhaps it came from the Hive Spirit?

The Hive Legend is passed on

"Each colony, and every bee, can learn and profit by experience" said a forager. "I, for example, well remember when all the apple and pear trees in the garden were in flower, and I worked hard as a house bee at receiving nectar from the field bees when they brought it home. The big apple tree beyond the grass, at the back of the hive, was as covered with pink blossom as it is now with leaves. I also remember when the bee-keeper opened the hive earlier in the season. These are memories, but they are not part of the Hive Legend. Such things never are. But when, in a few days' time, we go out with a swarm, that will be part of the Hive Legend, and each of us will know what to do when the time comes."

I already knew the Hive Legend on swarming, as we had been preparing for the event, and could repeat it to myself without hesitation.

We continued to consider other potential enemies. The Hive Legend also speaks of mice, who will move into a hive in the autumn and make a nest, living throughout the winter on honeycomb and clustered bees. They can easily destroy a colony that way. Another enemy, at its most dangerous towards the end of summer, is our distant cousin, the wasp. Wasps make their way into the hive to steal honey; and being bigger and stronger, have an advantage over us. They even kill and eat individual bees when they have a chance to do so.

I imagined that such things would not concern me. I was a summer bee, and would not be around when they happened. But I was wrong.

"You must learn about it, and pass it on to the generation that comes after you" I was told. "The Hive Legend must always be passed on to others. It must never be lost. The autumn and winter bees can only learn it from you."

I touched the bee who told me this, acknowledging my mistake, and went off to eat and in turn to feed the brood. The greater part of the night had already passed. It would be dawn soon.

"The enemy was a flying creature, very much bigger than a bee."

CHAPTER THREE

The Swarm

When I Next Visited The Royal Nursery, The Larvae, In their fifth day from hatching, were almost fully grown and their curved bodies nearly filled the bottom of each cell.

I spent most of the following night near to them, keeping them warm and talking to my fellow nurses about the changes which would soon be taking place.

As soon as the princesses' cells were sealed, the colony would enter the final stages before sending out the swarm. This would probably be the single most important event in the life of any one of us, and even of the colony as a whole.

As bees, we have two ways of obeying the ancient impulse of multiplying the race. One is to nurture the larvae that come from eggs laid by the Queen, giving birth to individuals. But there is also another way which gives life to new independent colonies by the time-honoured process of division. This is swarming.

The Hive Legend tells that the colony shares the old and the new. The bees that stay will keep the old home, but acquire a new Queen. Meanwhile, those whose adventure might seem at first to be the greater since they leave and find a new home, nevertheless keep part of the old life, too, since they retain our Queen.

Preparing for the swarm

I was not yet aware of a third way, when both the home and the Queen are changed, and all the old ties are cut, but was to learn of it later.

We waited together for the right time to seal the cells, aware of taking part in a pre-ordained cycle.

In the morning, when the hive became less crowded, I went to check that all was well with the young brood. When I came back to the princesses, I noticed that the tip of one cell was about to be sealed. I touched the larva inside, still lying in its pool of food, which she would soon no longer need. I helped to seal the cell, adding hair to the wax to make it strong and porous, and also allowing the occupant access to air. I loved all the babies for whom I cared, but this one was special, and on her would be based the whole future of the colony. She would outlive me many times over; and although, in reality, she was my sister, I could not help thinking of her as a mother, the future mother of the whole colony.

As the day progressed, preparations for the swarm were afoot. They took many forms. First of all, the Queen had to be prepared for a flight. She would not be capable of flying when in full lay, as she would be much too heavy. The way to reduce her weight was to reduce the number of eggs she carried by cutting down her food.

I became aware of all this when I joined her court for a while and sensed a difference of tempo, in the feeding of the Queen and in her egg-laying. Both took place with less of an urgency, and although we still loved and honoured her, other loyalties were now beginning to form.

Slightly less than half of the colony would be leaving. The excitement was general. I talked to many of my sisters about it. Each bee had to make her own decision, but she would also be influenced by the need of the colony and of the future swarm. Those that went out would have to be in a position to re-create an independent unit in the shortest possible time. Finding a place to live would be of paramount importance.

In the afternoon, I went on a short flight, circling several times above the hive, taking in the sunlit garden and the area beyond it. It was not the time to go any further. The babies still had to be fed. I saw older bees taking off in

Deborah decides to stay

all directions and returning empty-handed to the hive. Once inside, where I followed, one of them danced excitedly on the face of the comb. More came back with the same message. They had found good accommodation a little over a hundred yards away. Two other rival claims for a new home were being made by other returning scouts, but both were farther away, and possibly less suitable. It looked as if a consensus of opinion was forming about the destination of the swarm.

By evening, the other Queen cell had been sealed. I returned to my nursing. It was warm, and would have been a good time for evaporating honey, but very little had been brought in that day. Bees went about in little groups; and when I joined one of them, I soon found myself outside, on the alighting board. It was dusk. Small clusters of bees formed on the walls of the hive, and individual bees wandered between them, joining first one group, and then another, for conversation. I did the same. There was only one topic: whether to go or to stay. No one was obliged to do either. Each bee made her own decision, but it helped to talk it over with the others. We shared out food as we talked.

Many of the younger foragers should be prepared to go, we agreed, to keep up the strength of the swarm for as long as possible while it was becoming established. Wax workers were also most essential to the swarm, since they were to furnish the new home. Until they had made comb, not an egg could be laid, not a drop of nectar stored. Finally, as many youngsters as possible should be encouraged to leave, to take on the duty of nurses when the first eggs hatched in a few days' time.

A certainty began to form in my mind. I was staying. There was still a lot of brood to be nursed in the old colony, and I would give my allegiance to my new sister-Queen as she took over.

It was a strange, restless night. Because of the excitement, the warmth of the air and the overcrowding, many bees decided to sleep outside. A large cluster formed, hanging from the landing board, but there was also a lot of to-ing and fro-ing. Some came in, saying that it was pleasant sitting on the balcony, but that it did become a little chilly after a time. Others maintained that if one was well stocked-up with honey, the cooler air was no problem.

There was a problem, however, for some bees who became distracted by distant lights, and flew off into the night to investigate. They would be lucky if they survived alone till morning and found their way back.

Filling up with honey

The next day was the day of the swarm. We were anxious about the weather. When not busy nursing or eating, I popped out to look at the sky. There was not a cloud in sight. The alighting board and front of the hive were crowded. Some foragers were still going out to bring back nectar and pollen, but had difficulty in pushing their way through the waiting crowds on their return. I noticed that some of the pollen-gatherers, instead of rushing in to unpack, joined the group outside. The brilliant orange pollen of the rock rose in the baskets of one bee clearly stood out among the duller, green and grey pollens of acacia and raspberry. These bees were preparing to take this harvest with them as they went with the swarm.

As it was nearing noon, the prospective travellers went in turn to fill up to capacity with honey. This iron ration would be used as fuel for the flight, and also as raw material for wax-making in the new home. All those bees who were ready to go could not, of course, fit on the outside of the hive. As I went in and climbed back on to the comb, I saw that it was covered by a layer of bees that hung like heavy curtains extending underneath the combs, almost motionless and holding hand to foot, waiting. I walked over them towards the brood. Occasionally, a pair of antennae would touch mine, asking:

"Are you coming with us, Deborah?"

"No" I answered. "I am staying. Good luck!"

Above them, on the brood, waited the Queen, surrounded by her court. I was allowed to go through. I touched her in farewell, and received a parting

The signal to go

gift of Queen substance. I passed it on to others who were staying behind. All the bees around me shared out this last taste of the Queen. There was a marked difference in the Queen now. She was slimmer; and no longer busy laying eggs, she waited for the moment when, for the first time since her wedding flight, she would fly out into the sun. She must have looked like this as a young princess, I thought: relaxed and carefree.

Then it happened. I do not know who gave the signal, or perhaps there was no signal.

Anyway, it was time. The living curtains dissolved as the bees ran down the combs; and as they touched antennae for the last time, the message was passed, like an electric current:

"Go! Go! Go!"

I could not help it. The signal was overwhelming. When the Queen moved with her attendants, I went with them. We dropped down from the comb, ran along to the entrance and streamed out in a flood. We rose immediately high above the trees, circling round and round, in order not to lose sight of each other. The sky over the garden was suddenly black with bees, and still more poured out of the hive, drones among them.

The air vibrated with the humming of wings. It is a good thing that we see movement so well, otherwise there would have been countless collisions. As it was, we could move aside, passing so closely that our bodies felt only the rush of air from each other's wings. The moving cloud gradually condensed. A blackbird, on his way from one perch to another, flew into it, realized that something extraordinary was taking place, turned round and escaped in a state of panic.

The milling swarm began to move towards the right, away from the hive, but I felt that I must not follow. Instead, I found myself on the edge of the cloud, and then right outside it. I looked at the hive from above, and then at the swarm. Bees were beginning to settle on a pear tree about fifteen yards away. I could already see the dark mass of the hanging cluster through the cloud of ever-moving bees. I myself was drawn back to the hive. I was staying.

During the afternoon, we began to pick up the threads of normal routine. Not many nurses must have left, as there was little difference in the amount of work falling to each of us, but I was aware of meeting far fewer very young bees. These, the future nurses, had flown out with the swarm, leaving behind only the newborn, who walked about shakily on the brood combs, not yet able to use their wings. I introduced some of them to the colony, giving them food and encouragement.

A new hive appears

During the rest of that day and the night, more bees were born. By the time these reached the nursing age, there would be no brood left to feed, or very few. Since bees age chiefly through the effort of producing brood food, they would remain young for a comparatively long time.

That night, when we were all together again, it became more apparent that we had sent out a swarm. There was more room to move about: but the hive still seemed fairly full. There was, however, another kind of emptiness. We had no Queen. We compensated for this up to a point by frequent visits to the princesses, as yet unborn; and although they were sealed up in their cells, where they had already began the process of change, we could feel their living presence through the walls.

We worked, and we waited. As no more eggs were being laid, those house bees who had been left behind, did not feel as pressed to get cells ready for new occupants as soon as they became vacant. Instead, they took their time in cleaning and polishing them to perfection. Some would soon move on to nursing duties. I also felt that I was about to move on to something else: and for the second time in my life, I felt drawn to nursing older larvae, leaving the smallest babies in the care of my younger sisters.

The next day was brilliantly sunny. I flew out into the garden and rose high above the apple trees, always keeping the hive in sight. Its position had to be fixed in my memory, so that finding it again would soon become second nature. Looking down, I was extremely surprised to see something that looked exactly like our hive, but which had not been there before. It certainly seemed to be a hive, as many orientation flights were taking place in front of it: but I was glad that I could already pinpoint the entrance to *our* hive with great accuracy, and so would not confuse the two.

Our hive stood facing south-east. Before it were two apple trees, three yards away on either side. The new hive, two yards away, faced directly south.

Memorizing all the landmarks

Where had it come from? It was not put there by bees, of course, but something or someone must have put it there for the use of bees. Since it was just like ours on the outside, the inside was probably just like ours as well. It would be dry, easily kept clean, and easy to ventilate. The bees, occupying the new hive, would probably be very much like us, too. Perhaps the swarm had changed its mind and had taken up residence much closer than planned. But the bees, now flying to and from the hive, even if they had once been our sisters, had to be independent of us in every way.

I remembered part of the Hive Legend which had been passed around during the final night before the swarm went out.

"Once a swarm has left and clustered away from the parent hive around the Queen, it starts life anew, as another family. There is no going back, however hard things may be. The colony is born again at that moment, and old ties are cut."

"I must remember that there are two hives, and always return to the right one" I told myself.

I memorized all the landmarks. Beyond the apple trees, four yards away, grew a hedge. Farther away still, there was a wooden fence; and just behind it, a row of big trees, then a vast expanse of green grass. A roughly triangular area, between some bushes, was inviting, as a lot of small flowers stood out among the green. They were in our favourite colours: yellow, blue and mauve. There were some white flowers, too, which formed a broad swathe of delicate, creamy lace under the old hedge. But most of the grass was dull and uninteresting because, for some reason, no flowers grew in it.

Close by, before reaching the trees and the fence, there was a double cordon of raspberries, where I could see my sisters at work, gathering nectar and pollen. In the opposite direction, behind the hive, there was again a somewhat smaller area of grass, which ended in a solid shape, many times bigger than our hive, so that I would have had to rise much higher still to fly over the top. To one side of the grass, three more apple trees gave shade from the afternoon sun to the hives and the garden.

As I flew in increasing circles, I was also taking my bearings from the sun. The colour of the sky was graded from very deep blue away from the sun to very pale close to it. As the sun moved, the pattern of light moved with it, and I knew exactly which direction I was facing. By taking account of the light and the time, I would never become lost.

A heady mingling of scents

I was now followed home by several field bees who had been working on the raspberries, and who were laden with pollen and nectar. Since they had not far to fly, they could afford to collect huge loads. I felt that help was needed, and offered to take the nectar from one of them, leaving her to deal with the pollen. She opened her mandibles, and I inserted my proboscis between them to draw up the liquid. It had a delicious taste. As she transferred the load, we talked and exchanged views on the new hive.

"It probably is our swarm" she agreed. "I saw them going into the hive in the late afternoon. They were walking up to the entrance along a big, sloping ramp, which has now disappeared."

"Where did the hive come from?" I wondered.

"Bee-keepers put it there. I saw two of them, huge, all in white, carrying the hive parts and assembling them, then bringing a basket full of bees."

I remembered the white figure which had so frightened me by opening our hive some days ago, and still felt an intense dislike at the memory.

We finished the transfer of nectar, and for the first time in my life, my honey sac was completely full. I went up to the store, and there settled down to evaporate it little by little, running each droplet between my mandibles and proboscis several times, before adding it to a storage cell. A large group of bees was engaged in similar work. There were many more sources beside the raspberries, so the mingling of different scents was quite heady.

When I had finished my first batch, I went down again, offering my services to the incoming foragers. This time, I was given something quite different, with a heavy, sweet fragrance.

"This is robinia" came the information along the antennae of the worker, as she transferred the load. "A very big tree, covered with hanging bunches of white flowers."

Bees working on the robinia came at longer intervals, as the tree was quite far away; but the concentrated nectar was worth the effort, they said.

Working in the honey store

The honey harvest now came from many, scattered sources, providing a steady flow of varied scents and tastes. As I helped each bee to unload, she shared with me her knowledge of the flower from which it came. Some field workers were very resourceful, and returned proudly with something new, which they themselves had discovered. Such plants included the aromatic herbs – thyme, lovage, sweet cicely and others – their powerful fragrances making them even more valuable than the amount of nectar they offered would suggest. Thyme, especially, gave the honey a special quality. I rejoiced in the rich mixture.

Other bees formed small parties which specialized in the limited, but valuable food source of certain plants. One of these groups worked on the cotoneaster, which grew against a wall on the other side of the house. It was nearing the end of its flowering period; but the small, pink heads, like tiny cups, gave nectar of such intensity that it needed little evaporation. Another plant, even more generous in the amount of sugar which it offered, was coming into flower. This was borage, a dainty, upside-down flower of deep blue, seemingly created especially for bees. Indeed, its nectar fell little short of the strength of honey.

We worked late into the night, reducing the water contained in the nectar and turning it into honey by the addition of special substances. After some time, I realized that I had not been near the brood for most of the day. During my walkabout, I went in that direction. Other, younger bees were now looking after the babies, and everything was in order. I offered them some of my abundant honey, and felt a new richness of experience and contentment.

As my work in the honey store continued during the following day, I learned that a large proportion of the ready honey had in fact been taken by the swarm. It was a perfectly normal thing to do. Even when filled to capacity, a swarm starts life at a disadvantage in comparison to a settled family. I felt, however, that we would have to make up the losses, though I did not really know the reason. It was a natural thing for bees to gather nectar and turn it into honey; but so far I had not asked myself why so much of it was necessary.

Gathering winter stores

I put that question, somewhat hesitatingly, to the forager who was giving me her crop of nectar at the time. She must have been so taken aback that the movement of her antennae stopped abruptly, and she stood still on the comb.

"Don't you know?" she asked incredulously.

"Not really" I admitted.

"Have you not heard of winter?"

Immediately, I connected the Hive Legend with what we were doing. Bees cannot leave the hive for many days, and must live on winter stores. There was no need to ask more.

"We are gathering winter stores for those of us who must stay in the hive until spring" I said. I had answered my own question. Now I knew.

The other bee touched me again.

"How strange not to know why we must make honey" she mused.

I returned to my work with an added sense of purpose.

The nectar sources were not very abundant, but at least the weather was perfect, and the working day so long that these scarce resources could be used to the full. I took part in receiving nectar from the field bees, taking it up to the store and helping to evaporate it. The super-abundance of nectar which I was eating during the honey-making process was partly absorbed by my own body, again creating a sense of fulness. But this was a feeling different from that experienced at the start of my nursing career. That had been created mainly by eating pollen, and resulted in the production of bee milk for the babies. This time, the food was nectar.

When a cell of nectar was sufficiently evaporated, and its contents turned into honey, the cell had to be sealed. It then became evident why I had this sense of fulness. While working on the honey, my body quite independently began to produce wax, our universal building material, and small plates of it appeared on the underside of my abdomen. I was able to pick them up, chew each piece to a malleable consistency, and add a little wax to the outer wall of the honey cell. It was a pleasure to work in this way.

Slowly the capping grew, as one or another of us found her sliver of wax ready to use, until only a small dot of unsealed honey was left. Then one bee

The good of the wintering family

put the finishing touch by closing the gap. The honey was now safe. It would not spoil, as the wax cappings, unlike the cappings used for brood cells, were made to exclude air so that the contents of the cell would not absorb moisture and deteriorate in storage.

That night, once nectar brought in during the day had been evaporated, we formed our loose cluster. I was still wondering at the enormity of the task before us and at the amount of work that would have to be done in order to provide enough food for all the winter bees. I knew how quickly stores were used up in the colony. As usual, I turned to my elder sisters for explanation and reassurance. The oldest of them had been born only about fifty days earlier, but they already knew the complete Hive Legend which was our guide, and they repeated part of it to me.

"The wintering family is much smaller than it would be in summer. Only young bees, who are born in the autumn, are able to live through the whole of the winter until spring, and then build up the colony again. Eggs are laid and the brood reared when it may still be very cold, long before there are any nectar-giving flowers. To save stores for keeping this nucleus colony strong and to provide warmth for the first larvae to grow, it is better if older bees do not try to winter. Drones should be made to leave the hive once summer is over and no more nectar is likely to come in."

The last part came as a surprise. Admittedly, drones contributed little to the running of the hive, except for providing extra heat, and adding to the sense of well-being which came mainly from the Queen. It was unheard of to argue with the Hive Legend, but I found it difficult to accept unless I understood it.

"Must drones always go in the autumn?" I persisted. "Is there no way of keeping them?"

"Sometimes a very strong colony may keep some drones," came the answer, "but drones are an added burden in winter. It is better not to take risks, but to concentrate on the important things: stores and plenty of young workers. In any case, drones live about as long as summer bees. That is quite enough. Both workers and drones must be subjected to the good of the entire family."

"The surface was covered with leaves on which I could stand, without the danger of falling in, and drink."

Cooling the hive

I could not but agree with the wisdom of this. Nevertheless, I was rather glad that I would not be there in the autumn. I felt I would not have enjoyed the duty of forcing drones to leave the hive. The drones whom I knew and met in my daily life would not last so long either. We would all give way to a new generation of drones and workers while the summer lasted.

It was a strange in-between time. The swarm had left two days before, and the last of the eggs laid by our old Queen were hatching into larvae. A day later, not one egg was left.

Meanwhile, young bees were emerging, and the cells which they vacated were made ready for the next generation, but as yet stood empty. There was still work for the nurses; and occasionally, for want of anything else to do, I visited the older brood, but that work steadily diminished. A certain amount of nectar was coming in, but not that much.

We were all waiting for the new Queen to emerge, for fresh plants to come into flower, and for new duties which we could take on.

It became extremely hot. I spent a lot of my daytime hours taking my turn in ventilating the hive, until the temperature became so high that evaporating water from incoming nectar was not sufficient to cool the air, and some of us set out in search of water. One of the scouts showed us the direction.

Not too far away was a small pond, very conveniently sited. The surface was covered with leaves on which I could stand without the danger of falling in, and drink. Birds also came to drink at the pond, and some of them were light enough to stand in the centre of a big leaf: some splashed in the water.

We collected our supply of water, a honey sac full, and flew back to the hive to spread it out on all the surfaces. Those of us who also took on the task of standing with beating wings at the entrance, to create a draught, brought down the temperature of the hive, but became very hot ourselves. The best remedy for that was to fly out to fetch a new supply of water. Having your honey stomach full of coolness was a pleasant sensation in the heat. But I was told that in the early spring, when water is needed not to cool the hive, but to dilute stored honey to a usable consistency, it is an entirely different situation. Bees filling up with cold water are often so chilled that they cannot fly back to the hive. Many perish in that way, at a time when the colony numbers are often at their lowest, and no lives can be spared.

Perfect flying weather

But for the present, fetching water was only a pleasure. The pond was farther away than I had ever been, and the hive was just out of sight, but I could still see our trees and the general layout of the area.

It would have been an ideal time in which to make honeycomb, as wax must be worked at as high a temperature as can be obtained in the hive without damage to the brood. Unfortunately, we had little room in which to fit new combs. I helped with constructing the comb right under the ceiling or crownboard, where the old comb had been damaged when the hive was opened, but there was little space in which to build and the work was unrewarding. We would have liked to hang in huge festoons, holding on to one another by the claws on our feet, creating our own heat and our own building material, making a structure on which the form of the new nest would depend. Here, however, the structure was complete, and there was not much we could contribute. Besides, working upwards from existing combs was difficult.

Two days passed in this relatively unhurried fashion: days of heat, little in the way of harvest, and waiting. Our drones spent most of their time outside, revelling in the perfect flying weather. What marred our peace, though, was that the bee-catching bird was still occasionally seen, observing the entrance and making sudden dashes in an attempt to catch the returning bees, who were tired and full of nectar at the moment of landing. Our guards had to be on the alert, and usually succeeded in sending him off by sheer force of numbers: but we were annoyed at the intrusion.

The nights were pleasant. We took turns to sit out on the balcony after dusk, going in from time to time to help with the cooling of the hive. Towards the latter part of the night, when it suddenly became colder, we would go in, form a loose cluster around the brood, and talk.

As the day of the emergence of our new Queen drew near, the atmosphere became tense. We had two Queen cells, both perfect, but could have only one Queen. The problem would have to be resolved somehow.

The Hive Legend offered two possible solutions. Either the first princess

The first princess emerges

to emerge would tear down the cell of her younger sister and sting her to death – the only occasion on which a Queen ever uses her sting: or, if the colony so decided, she would leave with some of the bees in a second swarm, known as a cast, and bequeath the mother hive to her sister. We felt unsure as to which road to take, but felt the Hive Spirit would guide us when the time was ripe.

One evening, the waiting was over. Those bees who had been keeping watch over the Queen cells began to peel off the tip of a cell, so that a princess would find it easier to cut her way out. But even she, the future Queen, had to work at her release from confinement. We were given a running commentary, which spread from bee to bee throughout the hive.

First she cut a circle from the bottom of the large cell in which she had been hanging head downwards until, with a push, the door which was still attached in one place by a hinge, suddenly opened, and she slid out easily. The bees around received her, greeted her, and let her go. She had to find her own feet and learn how to use her body, like any one of us. She was fed, and allowed to explore at her own pace. There was only one place where she was not welcome: the other princess's cell, still guarded by a retinue of workers.

During the night, as the new princess explored, she showed that she was not just like one of us after all. She began to sing.

Her song was like piping, a single, long melodious note, which then broke into a staccato sequence. The sound reverberated around the hive, magnified by the wooden walls, reaching everywhere. Ordinary working sounds of the colony – the fanning of wings, the scraping of cells and the moulding of wax – paled into insignificance.

The princess rested for a few moments, and then began again. The first note was a loud, echoing call, and the following ones were repeated in quick succession, until finally they faded away. We all stopped to listen. She wandered from comb to comb, beginning each new song in a different place. Those of us who were free, turned towards the source of the sound. At one point, I found myself next to the singer, and offered her food. She took it, standing above me on her long, slim legs. She was so very young, yet so much depended on her.

She began the piping song again, and this time her sister answered. But the answering voice was muffled by the cell walls; it was far less vibrant, and on a lower note. The new princess followed the sound, and I went with her. We were met at the royal cell by a cluster of guarding bees, several bodies deep. The princess was jostled aside and not allowed through. I could feel that a decision had been made. Since there may not be two sister Queens in a hive, either the younger must die or the elder must leave. The young, unhatched princess was being looked after. So, it seemed, the one already born would be leaving.

This decision was much more sudden than the one concerning the original swarm had been. That had been meticulously prepared for days. This would be a matter only of hours. We were strong, the weather was perfect, we could afford another swarm. But those taking part would be cast into the unknown. This swarm would comprise a much smaller number of bees, and an unmated, unproven Queen. It might be several days before she could start laying eggs. The two royal sisters still talked in their fashion, one piping, the other sending out replies; but the younger would be confined to her cell until her rival left. It would therefore have to be soon.

This time I felt no hesitation. I was leaving. Wax-working bees had little to do in our mother hive, whereas with a cast the scope seemed endless. We had no idea where we would be going, there was no time to investigate. It was a risk, an adventure.

Preparations for the cast were in hand from early morning. I went out to see what it was like outside. The grass was sparkling with dew, and close to the ground a thin layer of mist formed as the moisture evaporated under the rays of the early morning sun. The hive exit was just above that layer. As the sun moved, to touch areas until then hidden in the shade, I saw them enveloped in steam. With every moment that passed, the process became faster, and the sun grew stronger.

I returned to the hive to feel the mood of my sisters. Touching antennae with several bees of my generation, I knew that we were all of one mind, and would soon be going in order to contribute our wax-working skills until such time as they were no longer needed. Some of the youngest bees, born since the first swarm went out five days ago, would also be leaving, to take their turn as nurses as soon as eggs were laid. A lot of the present nurses, who had less and less employment since there was now practically no open brood apart from some drones who stay at the larval stage a day longer, would be leaving too. They would be invaluable to us.

We went into the honey area to fill up with stores that would tide us over the next three days or so, and waited for the weather to warm up before going. Our young Queen was restless. As a new princess, she had waited with less ceremony for the signal to go than her mother had done, having as yet no court around her. She rubbed sides with the workers. Some drones, interested in the course of events, kept near her, clearly intending to join the swarm. A few of them would perhaps mate with the Queen, and thus become fathers of the future colony.

It was still more than an hour to noon when the urge to go overwhelmed us. We poured out of the hive in a stream, rushing upwards, hovering above the hive until we formed a swirling cloud over the garden. This time, I joined in wholeheartedly, without hesitation.

As we circled, waiting for all the bees that were going with us to assemble, the cloud consolidated, and then began to roll away from the hive. The tree chosen by this cast was an old apple tree near the house which, as I had heard in my youth from older bees, was covered in spring with large, pink blossoms that provided a feast of nectar. Now it was leafy and cool in the heat, and we would be able to wait there in comfort until our scouts came back with the news of a place to live.

We settled quickly, choosing a fork in the tree to take some of the strain off the bees that supported the main weight, and formed a cluster, hanging hand to foot. This was a temporary, but nevertheless good arrangement.

We carried with us loads of pollen and nectar, all that was necessary to prosper in a new home. Our young Queen was with us. The journey into the unknown had begun.

CHAPTER FOUR

The Old Ties are Cut

Although Homeless, We Were Already A New Unit. I Felt the truth of the Hive Legend. "Once a swarm has left and clustered around the Queen, it begins a new life, and the old ties are cut".

Some of the foragers, eager to take up their usual routine and feeling that to sit still when so much had to be achieved was a waste of time, went out in search of pollen. They would soon be back, and we would not move for some time yet.

Older foragers who knew the area well, also went off to investigate. They began to return, each with a different message apparent in her dance, but none of it very exciting.

I followed one of the dances, and was led to a place quite close, in the wall of the house. It had several parallel openings to the outside, but would not be big enough as the colony grew. There was no room to expand; so on returning to the cluster, I was not inclined to recommend it.

Another of my sisters had just come back from a similar investigation. They had found a structure with plenty of room, she said, but it was completely open to the sky. She was an older bee, who had experienced rain several times, and had a poor opinion of a home without a roof. Besides, the place smelled of smoke and was full of soot which would have to be removed.

Those bees who were sufficiently interested to go and investigate other proposed places had also come back unconvinced. We would have liked a home as good as the one we had left; but any enclosed space with an entrance could be made into a home, providing it was the right size.

I was just then inside the cluster, so it was a great shock to feel suddenly a violent shaking of the branch on which we were hanging.

Many of the bees supporting our weight had to let go, and we fell, but not all the way to the ground. A deep, round object had appeared underneath us, and some of us fell into that. It had small, regular holes all over the walls and bottom, and smelled faintly of wood. As we disentangled our feet, we either walked up its walls to the open top, trying to regain our previous position in the tree, or took to the air instead. We were furiously angry at this interference.

I had a sudden glimpse of the white-clad bee-keeper standing in the tree, surrounded by my buzzing sisters. The unmistakeable smell of sting venom was everywhere, and it aroused me to even greater anger. We would not allow this creature to break up our cluster, even if several of us had to die in its defence. It was a basic law: swarming bees must stay together at all cost. This time, however, it was not my turn to sting. I calmed down and settled back on the branch. The peace had been broken. But the bee-keeper disappeared.

Our cluster was now re-formed in the same place. Guard bees remained in the air, patrolling around in case of a new danger. This came sooner than expected, but in a different form: a smell of smoke. It caused less fear in the open than it would have done in a hive, since we felt free to fly away if the absolute necessity arose. There was not much of it, however, and it seemed to be coming from underneath us.

Over our heads a basket appeared, the open end invitingly above the cluster. Trying to avoid the smoke as far as possible, we began to move slowly upwards without losing contact. The inside of the basket was cool and shady, and there were only small chinks of light showing through its walls and top. We re-formed our cluster in comfort along one of the walls, which gave an excellent foothold. The smell of smoke was no longer there.

I felt a gentle movement as we were taken down and placed on the ground. There was a gap at the bottom of the basket, wide enough to allow us

"Over our heads a basket appeared, the open end invitingly above the cluster."

to come and go. The basket, in fact, offered better protection. What's more, our Queen was safe.

The next thought was to make sure that none of us had been left behind. There may have been some bees still sitting in the tree, drawn back to the lingering scent of the swarm, and they would have to be called down to join us. A few bees had already positioned themselves at the entrance to the basket, facing towards it and stretching their back legs, so that the abdomen pointed upwards and exposed the scent gland near its tip. This showed as a pale crescent and exuded a strong wave of bee scent, which was dispersed by the vigorous fanning of wings. It was a wonderfully reassuring smell.

"Here we are" it said. "Come and join us!"

It must have reached far afield, as more and more bees were descending from the tree and walking into the basket. Some joined the fanners at the entrance to enhance the message even further. Not all, however, were sufficiently careful to fan in the right place. There was an alternative call coming from above, and I went up to investigate.

Some bees were fanning strongly on top of the basket, with the result that a few nervous-looking individuals landed there but could not find a way in. I tried to point both the callers and the seekers in the right direction, touching their antennae and reassuring them that there was a way in, but lower down. They began to move; and once they had found their bearings, ran in with visible relief.

By now, the field bees who had risked seeking pollen were beginning to return, and I joined the fanners to make sure that as few as possible would be lost. One of them returned proudly with an almost black pollen load, which I had never seen before. It came from the poppy, she said. There was, of course, nowhere that it could be unloaded, and she had to look after it and carry it around until we had built some comb. For the moment, she could not go foraging again.

By now, it was early afternoon, and we were hoping to see our scouts return with the message of a perfect home, but nothing definite was reported. Each bee dance told a different story.

I was inside the basket and walked upwards on the cluster. My sisters began to settle down happily; and a few wax workers, eager to begin construction of new combs, had already made a start on the inside of the roof. The shape of cells was beginning to emerge at the point where the cluster was attached. We all knew, of course, that a home should be proof against wind and water if bees are to live well through the winter. The light basket was hardly that. So far, however, it was the best home we had.

A violent shaking

Clearly, we were not going to be left in peace. The basket was lifted yet again, very slowly and gently this time, so that not a bee was dislodged from her foothold, and carried for a few moments. There was no longer a floor to it, daylight came from below on to the cluster, and we were hanging over empty space. Then, without any warning at all, the basket was shaken violently. Once again, we fell in a tangled heap, and the shock of it was such that each one of us buzzed loudly in protest as she came down.

I felt myself lying on a thick layer of my sisters, all of them moving, and there were others above me. We were slipping off each other, spreading out sideways under the force of gravity, trying to regain our feet. When at last I managed to stand, I found myself on a sloping surface. As usual, not knowing where I was, I felt instinctively that the best way to go was upwards. The bees above me were beginning to move, and the layer of bodies on top of me became gradually thinner. I stood still, awaiting my turn, while others moved forward in a harmonious wave, often treading in each other's tracks. Somewhere ahead was our Queen, and once more there came a scent of calling bees, urging us to assemble. When I could walk freely, I again took the upward direction. Ahead, on top of the slope, was a narrow, dark opening through which my sisters were pouring: a living, glistening tide. The nearer they were to it, the less they hesitated, and the faster they went. I looked around. Some bees, isolated on the fringes of the board, had hardly moved, but sat motionless, as if disorientated. I turned towards one and touched her, arousing her from this stupor.

"Come on" I said with my antennae. "You'll be left behind. Don't waste time."

It was all the encouragement that was needed. She started without hesitation and caught up a few others who were also on their way up. I went from one laggard to another, urging them on, and joined the last one, walking together with her into the hive.

The new home felt so familiar that it must have been a hive. There were frames containing thin sheets of wax, a foundation started by someone else, the shapes of cells clearly marked, but very shallow. A lot of work would be needed to turn them into finished comb. But I felt elated. I had all the tools for building comb: mandibles and forelegs for moulding wax, and a good store of honey which my body would turn into the building material. Now I would have endless scope to use them.

The swarm cluster was now beginning to turn into a wax-building cluster as we raised the temperature inside it. No time would be wasted. By the time our Queen was mated and ready to lay eggs, we would have beautiful new comb prepared for her.

I hung happily near the top, feeling the rising heat and the weight of my sisters hanging below me. My wax glands were beginning to respond, and after a while I was able to scrape carefully two thin, transparent slivers of wax from my body. I began to mould them with my mandibles.

Choosing one of the incipient cells, I added my wax, making a start at the building of a cell wall. Then came another pair of wax scales, and another. There were four pairs altogether, after which I had to wait for my glands to manufacture another batch. When I had used up all eight, and the wall felt more prominent by a tiny fraction, I went back into the main cluster again, contributing my body heat to our common furnace.

I was totally absorbed in the work. There was nothing else worth doing for the present. We could not eat: there was nothing to eat, and anyway we were still full of stores taken before swarming. And there was no brood. We were not inclined to rest other than in the wax cluster, and here the resting time was used for producing wax. As our own personal honey stores were being used up, field bees offered us their own, thereby unburdening themselves and making room in their honey stomachs for fresh nectar. At one point, a bee came to tell us that it was evening and getting dark. We worked on: the comb was taking shape. The next time I went to add my wax to the structure, the cell being built was already deep. I could now enter it completely and smooth the walls from the inside, using my own body dimensions as a measure to ensure the size was exactly right.

The weather interrupts

We worked on through the night, producing wax, working it and adding it to the comb, then resting. The night was hot and more humid than usual. Our Queen was being fed, her wing muscles were strengthening, and we hoped to have her out of the hive and on her mating flight as soon as possible. Until her first eggs were laid, we were extremely vulnerable. If there were no eggs, there was no possibility of raising a new Queen; and, as the Hive Legend says, there is no going back.

As the night went on, we became nervous. There was something in the air. Whatever my antennae touched felt charged with electricity, and the harmony of our work on the combs became disrupted. It was difficult to communicate. Messages were easily misunderstood; and instead of helping, we began to hinder each other in the process of building.

It was nearly dawn. We had a good area of comb finished, and it extended throughout the five central frames. The patch of completed cells was much larger on the central wax sheet, becoming progressively smaller towards the outside, and the whole had a roughly circular shape, somewhat similar to our natural cluster.

The sun, however, did not appear as expected. About the time when it should have been seen over the horizon, bringing with it a new, perfect day, the first in our new home, we heard a distant roll of thunder. It came again, becoming nearer and more pronounced, until a terrible crash close by shook the hive and disorganized our work. We hung together, but without any further attempt to build.

The thunder went on, to be followed by a downpour of rain. Our alighting board was drenched and tiny droplets splashed inside on to the floor of the hive. The temperature fell more sharply than it normally does at dawn. There was one consolation in all this – we had a good hive. What would have happened to us up in the tree, or even inside the basket, was not pleasant to

Preparing comb for the brood

contemplate. We came more closely together, after the initial shock of the storm, and enjoyed each other's company again. The first violence had passed, but the rain continued to fall steadily, settling into a rhythm.

We now went back to our building work, still having enough food to produce wax. The spherical structure of the finished combs was expanding continuously. Those bees with remains of honey in their sacs began to deposit it at last in the newly provided cells, leaving enough space in the centre for the brood. It was an odd feeling to be in a hive with no babies at all, not even sealed brood. A whole dimension of life was missing, but we were all the more keen to have the nursery ready for when the time came.

Only worker cells were being constructed. Whoever it was who had started to prepare the wax sheets before we arrived in the hive had made no provision at all for drone cells, which are much larger. Had we wanted to do so, we could have chewed away part of the wax and laid foundation for drone cells; but we had no desire to change the original plan in order to build them. We felt that we must concentrate on creating a prosperous colony as soon as possible to ensure survival, and to start producing drones at this stage would have stretched our resources too far.

The steady rain continued all day. Leaving the hive was out of the question. An older bee who came up to the building area to supply us with more honey said that two or three foragers had taken the risk and gone out in the afternoon – there are always some who do not count the odds – and they had not come back. After this, word went round that no one was to leave the hive until the weather improved. We could not afford to waste lives. There would be no new bees born to the colony for about a month.

Night came again, the second in our new home. As we rested in the cluster between bouts of work, we began to take stock of the situation. On the whole we were optimistic, maintaining that rain could not go on for ever. But what was the best course to take? Should we go on building as fast as we had done, and risk using up all the honey we had in the process? Or should we be more careful? We had brought with us enough for about three days, and at least half of that had already gone in the great spurt of activity. On the other hand, the very fact that we had decided to leave with a cast entailed risk. It was now too late to be careful. We might as well take up the challenge and count on providence to supply the need, and to give us good weather before it was too late.

A lesson in survival

The night passed, and so did the next day, with no visible change outside, except that the wind rose even more and it became colder. We had continued to work, and most of the available space was now filled with beautiful new comb. There was, however, almost no food left. It had all been turned into wax. We clustered together, deciding finally to abandon the task of building and to share out the remaining food as fairly as we could, taking great care that the Queen should have all that she needed. None of us had ever before experienced real destitution, hunger of the whole family, which was now very close. All we knew about this sort of situation was contained in the Hive Legend. But in our case that source of wisdom on which we always relied was, for the first time ever, singularly unhelpful. This frightened us even more.

"A colony faced with a long stretch of bad weather must first cut down the food given to the Queen, to stop her from laying eggs", ran the Hive Legend.

This did not apply to us, as our Queen was not yet laying.

"Rather than let the whole family die, brood-feeding should stop to keep the adult bees alive. When there is no other choice, the brood can be sucked dry to provide food for the bees."

But we had no brood to sacrifice as a last resort. "If a colony is starving, the Queen should be the last to die."

We were certainly prepared to feed our Queen and keep her alive to the last. It was the only part of the Hive Legend which was relevant to our current situation, but it was also the least helpful. She would not survive long without us in any case. We wanted to find a way to save the whole family, not to set up an order of dying. Still, we knew that, unlike the parent colony, a cast was expendable. That also was part of the Hive Legend. All we could do was sit still in order to conserve our energy, and wait.

When day came, we sat quiescent in the cluster on the beautiful, new comb. The cells which once contained a little food were now empty again and licked clean. The rain went on, monotonously drumming against the hive. It could not rain for ever, we had thought. Perhaps we were wrong. Perhaps it could. There was no part of the Hive Legend about rain that never stopped, but there was a legend about the death of whole colonies. Even though each of us was individually quite willing to die for the good of all, the death of the colony would be hard to accept. A few of my weaker sisters were already beginning to drop off the cluster on to the hive floor.

It was probably late morning when we felt and heard a noise near the hive, over and above the sound of the wind and the rain. Something knocked against the roof and walls. Then a faint light and a draught of damp air came from above as a hole was uncovered in the ceiling. I and a few others who were near the top of the cluster looked out to check what was going on. Large drops of water splashed around us, and one drenched my thorax and wings as it made a direct hit. In spite of this, I had time to see a human hand holding some unknown object, and behind it the rest of the bee-keeper.

Being wet, I was unable to fly out and sting; and, strangely, I had no particular desire to do so. After a moment, it was already too late: the opening was covered once more. I paused on the top bar of a frame directly underneath the place where the hole had been, wiping the water from my eyes and body, and had just finished doing so when another big drop unexpectedly splashed on my head. As it touched my antennae, I froze in disbelief. It was sweet, like strong nectar. It was food!

We could not go out to gather food because of the appalling weather, and in some strange way food had come to us instead. There was no part of the Hive Legend, as far as I knew, to explain such a happening. I walked up on to the ceiling and found that, from the portion of it where the hole had been, there now hung droplets of sweetness, waiting to be collected. Some of my sisters were there before me, and were already drinking.

I found a droplet of my own and thrust my proboscis against it, drawing it in with quick movements of my whole body. My honey sac was soon filled, yet the droplet was still there, as if inexhaustible. We ran down to the cluster and opened our mandibles wide, offering the food to others. In a

"It came from our beloved borage. This upside-down, blue flower had been well protected from the rain."

Newly-found riches

few moments, the whole colony was in a state of high excitement. Help had come just in time to save us.

Other bees who tasted the food went up to see for themselves and to bring down more. In a short time, everybody had a share. Some thought of going down to see if those bees who had dropped off the cluster on to the floor had really died, or had just become too weak to hold on. About half of them were still alive, and they quickly revived when we offered food. There was still more of it to be collected.

This food was unlike anything with which I was familiar. It had a bland taste, pure sweetness, and had no hint of the flower from which it could have come. But that did not matter. It provided energy, warmth, and perhaps, if there was enough, further building material.

We continued to bring it down, and again put it aside for later use in the cells of our comb. The rest of the day passed happily, although trying to evaporate our newly-found riches was difficult in the damp atmosphere. The work kept us busy during the following night, too. But this time there was little clustering and no talk of death. Towards morning, as I was taking my turn at the storage cells, rolling each droplet of syrup on my proboscis as part of the process of turning it into honey, word came from above that no more of the sweet liquid was available. The bee who reported this said that she had finally inserted her proboscis right into one of the little holes from which the drops had come, and found nothing but air. All the others were empty, too.

We were not unduly worried, however. We now had some food in store, and perhaps help might come our way again. Being in much better spirits, we no longer believed in endless rain. Soon the sun would come out, and we would be able to go and collect our own nectar from flowers.

A feeling of anticipation

It was still raining, but less heavily than before, and there was now more light in the atmosphere. Surely the weather was going to change soon. We were impatient, as there was now little else we could do inside the hive. Then, for the second time, the inexplicable did happen. The hive roof was again taken off, and the hole over our heads was again covered with the surface that gave drops of syrup. We were no longer desperate, but were glad of the work which it provided in taking down and evaporating the gift. This time, we could afford to use some of it for wax-making, and formed the cluster again in order to extend the combs right up to the edges of the foundation sheets, filling all the available space. The syrup helped us to produce wax just as nectar did. All we needed was to drink the sugar solution.

By the following morning, there was a feeling of anticipation in the colony. The rain had stopped. I looked out on to the alighting board. The sun was rising over the trees, towards the left side of the entrance. It was pale, and did not yet give any appreciable warmth; but it was days since I had seen the sun, and I rejoiced at the sight. Everything around was still very wet, and the sun's rays were reflected from gleaming surfaces and from drops of water attached to every leaf, every blade of grass.

Very soon, field workers began to push past me on their way out, and I saw that they were all making orientation flights before venturing any distance. Slightly later, I also decided to go out. I left the hive with assurance; after all, I had made many flights earlier. But in the air, I suddenly felt a curious void in my knowledge. I no longer possessed a map in my head: and before I had time to realize it, I found that I had turned towards the entrance, just as if I were a youngster on my first day out, and began the basic, sideways, swinging flight. I was somehow aware of having done it before in just the same way, but now I belonged to another family.

Circling the hive

All my previous orientation flights came only as a vague memory, and there was a sense of unreality about them. They did, however, shorten the time necessary to reconstruct an inner map, and I was soon circling over the hive, higher and higher.

The hive stood facing east. Before it, but at an angle, stood two apple trees. To the left were two other hives, one facing south-east, the other south. It was most important to remember the direction which each of them faced in order not to go into a wrong hive. I continued to expand my map: and as each of these positions was learnt, I felt that I had known it all before, the new experience serving to reinforce the old one and to bring it forward in my memory. Only certain details were new.

The picture was quickly building up again. Beyond the apple trees was a hedge; then, further away a fence, and on the other side of it, some big trees and an expanse of grass. In the opposite direction, there was a house, a lawn, and three apple trees on the side of the lawn. That view I also recognized as something once known and forgotten.

Sufficiently sure of my bearings, I then went back to the hive, to help my sisters tidy up. Firstly, those bees who had died during the last few days had to be taken away. A few, for whom the syrup had come too late, were still lying on the floor. I walked up to one of the bodies and dragged it to the exit with the help of one of my sisters. Then I engaged four of my feet in holding the burden and took off with some difficulty, standing on my back legs only. But once airborne, I found I could fly quite a long distance before dropping it. It was much better to do that, I thought, than simply to push whatever I was clearing away from the alighting board. Such a lazy habit would lead to a mountain of debris by the entrance, which would be unpleasant. Several bees put their energies into this; and between us, we made short work of the cleaning.

I stopped on the alighting board to look out, and was quite happy to do just that. There was no brood in the hive, which meant that we did not have to stay inside in order to keep it warm; but we had to be careful not to allow any bees from the other two colonies, which were much stronger and more numerous, to come into our hive and perhaps steal the syrup which to us was invaluable.

Established as an independent colony

I stood in the guarding position, front feet off the ground, on the alert, checking bees as they came in. Some were simply returning from their orientation flights, and it was obvious from their behaviour that this was their home. Others were already bringing in pollen. We had no pollen in our hive as yet, only the small amount which the cast had managed to collect and bring on the day of the swarm, but it would be essential food for the nurses to feed both the Queen and the babies as soon as they were hatched. We still had our syrup, so there was less urgency to collect nectar. Anyway, there was very little nectar to be had. Perhaps the rain had washed it all away, or water had become mixed with it, making it so thin that it was not worth collecting. We would have to wait a while before all the excess water would be evaporated by the heat of the sun, and flowers returned to normal. Right now, it was still not warm enough for that.

It did, however, become warmer as the day went on. I was once more back in the hive, helping to evaporate the last of the syrup, when a field bee returned triumphantly with the first of the nectar. It came from our beloved borage. This upside-down, blue flower had been well protected from the rain; and even though the nectar was not yet up to full strength, it was much sweeter than some others could ever be, even at their best. We were becoming established at last as an independent colony.

Early in the afternoon, I met our Queen, and she asked me for food. I gave her some partly-processed nectar, as I sensed that what she needed at this stage was energy for her observation flight.

"I shall be leaving soon" she said to me as I touched her. "I am told that the air is quite warm enough."

I delivered the royal message to the bees around me, and found that some of them already knew. Indeed, the news was spreading with such speed that, by the time I reached the hive exit, there was already a small crowd there, waiting with anticipation.

Panic as never before

Suddenly I sensed a danger, one that I had met before. A bird was hopping a yard or so from the hive, a calculating look in its eye. I recalled the bird who used to catch bees, and this one appeared identical. It still kept its distance, but could attack quite unexpectedly at any moment.

"What a time for it to come, just as our Queen is about to leave!" we thought. There was a quick consulation.

"Force of numbers" I said. "That is it. We must all fly out and put ourselves between the Queen and the danger."

Several bees flew out. Some turned towards the hive, as if making an orientation flight themselves: others circled around it. The air was really warm now, and the sun brighter than before. I stayed a little longer at the exit, only to see that the Queen had just come out, stopping momentarily at my side. She was long and slim, and golden in colour. She may never have to fly as far a worker bee, and would probably tire more quickly, but she was certainly a very strong flier, I thought, as she took off at great speed. I followed her with my eyes, but she was soon lost among the other bees in the air. Safety in numbers: this applied well to the present circumstance.

A lot of other bees now came out and stopped beside me. If the bird wanted to catch a bee, it had a choice of any one of us, so long as the Queen remained safe. I spoke to a sister who was also following the Queen's flight.

"A Queen does not have to remember much of the Hive Legend. It is enough that we know it" she said to me. "But before she left, we made sure she remembered this part, as it refers to her more than to anyone else. A bee, and above all a Queen, must always return to the right hive".

There was a flutter of huge, feathery wings. The bird dashed forward and picked off the bee who had been talking to me. I jumped into the bird's face, but it was too late. The bird retreated under a tree to eat her.

"The Queen!" I thought, turning back to the hive. "Where is the Queen?" I felt panic as never before. Thankfully, at that moment she landed, flying almost straight down from the sky, and folding her wings which appeared shorter than ours because of the length of her body. She quickly went in. The crowd, which had been waiting nervously outside, followed her. A few of us, meanwhile, stayed behind until more of our sisters came back to relieve us on guard duty. The bird was still around, hopping under the trees, one eye on the hive entrance. A returning drone was captured by the bird on landing and taken away. We were all relieved that our Queen was safely inside. But she would have to go out again at least once, before her main mating flight.

The Queen prepares to leave

As I went in, I could see that the Queen was preparing to leave immediately after a short rest and a little nourishment. It was dangerous, but she was determined, so the only thing any of us could do was to create a diversion. In fact, as we congregated on the alighting board, the bird was nowhere to be seen; but we were not taking any chances, and the front of the hive was almost covered by bees.

When the Queen took off, I flew up at her side, but was quite unable to produce the same speed, and she quickly left me behind. I joined other bees, circling at treetop height, and could spot her from time to time as she overtook me at greater speed, flying in wider and wider circles, taking in the garden and its surroundings, and, I hoped, the other two hives as well, before swooping down to return home. I followed more slowly, and found her already settled and being fed by other bees.

Some of the rest of that day was spent in processing the nectar that was coming in. But my chief contribution lay in ventilating the hive, as I was drawn more and more to the entrance rather than to the honey store area. The outside held far more attraction for me.

At night, we clustered. After all those days of rain, it became chilly when the sun went down. We talked of tomorrow. News was passed round that the Queen thought she would soon be quite ready for her mating flight. She knew how much we longed to become a real colony, with brood and a laying Queen. There was only one more hurdle: the flight itself.

This was the mating sign

When at last the time came for the event, again in the early afternoon, all those present in the hive escorted the Queen out, either staying at the exit, or following her into the air. Our drones also followed, each visibly determined to catch up with the Queen. The mating would take place high up above the trees. Here, there would be many more drones around, ready and waiting for her arrival. The Hive Legend said that those who mated with her would die. They would be giving their life for the continuation of a family – not necessarily their own. We, being worker bees would not witness the event.

The speed at which the Queen flew was much greater than our own, and drones were stronger fliers still. We had no control over what happened so high above. It was far higher than we normally flew ourselves. Up there, maybe there were other dangers; other birds who hunted on the wing; but perhaps the number of drones around her would shield the Queen, just as the number of workers down below would do when she returned.

The bird hopped here and there under the trees. We waited tensely, walking about on the front wall of the hive. If the Queen came back, we would expand and prosper, giving all our energies to the common cause. If she did not, all our hard work would come to nothing and the colony would be destined to die.

The Queen reappeared as suddenly as she had gone, trailing behind her a piece of tissue remaining from the last drone who had mated with her. This was the mating sign. Young bees pulled it off, and we escorted her inside, forgetting for the time being all our problems. Our Queen was safe. Nurses came up to feed her and to take over her care. She now needed the most nutritious of milk for the development of her eggs. She was about to begin her life's work.

CHAPTER FIVE

Winning Through

RETURNING FIELD BEES WERE NOW BRINGING BACK GREAT loads of pollen. It was a very long, warm afternoon. As they scraped the pollen out of their baskets, I took part in packing it into the cells. Using my head to consolidate a load, I felt a taste and smell which aroused my curiosity.

"Poppies" said the harvesting bee. "There are great masses of them, just for the taking. I'll show you where."

We surrounded her with interest, and she ran downwards along the surface of the comb, wagging her tail vigorously from side to side. The dance was repeated, again and again. We followed her, trying not to lose contact. The message was clear.

"Fly directly away from the sun, for about two hundred yards."

It was time for me to make a direct contribution to the colony's welfare, and what better way than to bring in the pollen which was so essential at the moment. I went up to the uncapped honey cells for a quick drink, then ran down the comb, dropped on to the floor, wiped the remains of pollen from my eyes, and went out. I could still smell the pollen where it had touched my antennae.

The route indicated ran parallel to the back fence of the garden and over several other gardens, each with a patch of grass in the centre. Great masses of them, she had said. At about the right distance from home, there was indeed a mass of flowers, bee-violet in colour. I came down to investigate. Yes, the huge flower-heads, waving about on soft, slender stems, showed inside a mass of black anthers, and when I entered one of the flowers, the smell was unmistakeable. Even in this single flower, there was more pollen than one bee could possibly hope to gather and carry away. As I moved, it stuck to the hairs on my body, and I began to take up lots of it. I was wallowing in the pollen. My eyes were covered with it, and I could hardly see. It had, however, to be brought back to the hive under control, in my pollen baskets, not all over my body. For that, I would have to leave the flower and hover in the air beside it.

I moistened my forelegs with my tongue, and wiped the dry pollen from my eyes and face. Now I would be able to see again. I cleaned my antennae, also covered with pollen, using my antennae brushes; and then, with my middle legs, I wiped the pollen from my thorax, and used my hind legs to collect it.

Then came the packing. I rubbed my legs together in the air, scraping the pollen from the brush on one leg with the rake on the other, and squeezing it through the pollen press and into the basket. It was the first time in my life that I had attempted to go through this complicated series of movements. When I patted my pollen baskets with my middle legs, they did not appear to be as full as I had hoped. Inadvertently, some of the dry pollen had been lost in the transfer. Next time, I would have to dampen in even more.

Once again, I dived into the flower, covering my body with the powdery substance. This time, when I hovered to pack it, I took great care to use enough nectar from my honey sac so that the resulting pollen paste was quite sticky. Checking them, I found the baskets were now definitely far fuller. I needed several return trips to have anything resembling a full load, however. But after all, it was my first day, and it had not gone too badly.

I went back to the hive and unpacked this, my first pollen harvest. I placed it in a cell which already contained some pollen, pressing it down myself, using my head, as everyone else around appeared to be equally busy. There was still enough of the day left to go out again, and I continued to gather the black pollen, having made sure that I had enough nectar with me to moisten and consolidate each load. The poppies, although so generous with pollen, contained no nectar at all.

An embarrassing mistake

The sun had begun to go down, and shone diagonally across the garden in which the poppies grew. As the light changed, the flowers became less visible, their beautiful bee-violet turning to black. At last, I was no longer attracted to them, but did not yet feel the need to go back and rest. I looked around. In the hedge in front of the hive, growing right through it and reaching the open top, were some climbing roses. Their large, white, single flowers, open to the evening sky, stood out clearly in the slowly descending dusk. I was drawn to them and went to investigate.

Bees were still working inside some of the blooms, also collecting pollen, which in this instance was dull orange in colour. Before darkness fell, I would make one more outing, I decided, but it would be essential to work quickly. Trying to cut down the time necessary for packing the pollen, I discovered that the rose petals were much more solid than those of the poppies. If I suspended myself from the edge by one front leg, I could hang inside the flower and use the remaining five legs quite efficiently to scrape the pollen off my body into the baskets, thus cutting down the need to hover. I also found the roses offered a little nectar, which could be used to dampen the pollen.

The sun had set long ago, and dew had already begun to fall when I finally abandoned work to go home. I flew down on to the alighting board and began to go in, when I sensed that something was wrong. A bee approached; and when she touched me, I felt that she was a stranger. I had obviously ceased to concentrate, and had inadvertantly gone into the wrong hive. I bowed my head in apology, and backed away, not waiting to be thrown out. It was very embarrassing to have made that mistake at my age. I was over three weeks old, a forager, and I had behaved like a baby.

Thankfully, I returned home, checking a few times by flying to and fro that this really was the right place before going in. My rose pollen was put on top of a black load. A younger bee came up to help me with pressing it in. I sat down to clean myself of the remaining grains, especially my head and eyes,

Sharing in the Queen substance

and so swayed from side to side, asking for help. The young bee responded to the grooming dance and obliged, licking around the base of my wings and the awkward area between thorax and abdomen, which was still clogged with both types of pollen which I had been collecting. She ate the pollen grains, preparing herself for the nursing duties which would soon be needed, and offered me some nectar in return. A little earlier, she told me, she had been feeding the Queen.

Mixed with the flavour of nectar, there was also Queen substance, which my younger sister had obtained from our Queen as she was feeding her: but now for the first time it contained something which I had not tasted for a long while, not since I was quite young. After the uncertainty of the previous week, the hunger, and the fear that the Queen might be lost on her mating flight, the knowledge that all was well with our family at last filled me with a deep contentment. As I knew from the Hive Legend: "Only a mated Queen produces this substance which unites the colony in a special way". I told the other younger bee about it.

"Yes, the Queen had a new taste when I licked her" she agreed happily. She was too young to have had this experience before, as she had been born well after the swarm had left with our old Queen.

That night, I was near the Queen for a while, as she was being fed and licked by the nurses, and shared in the Queen substance again. The Queen now moved around very little, but sat calmly in the night-time cluster. Perhaps her attention was directed inwards, to the changes which were taking place in her body, or perhaps she was just resting. In the nature of things, in spite of all our love for her, the Queen always stands rather apart from the rest of the colony.

Next morning, it was still cool, but the slanting rays of the rising sun caught the entrance of our hive and roused us to a new day. It would have been more difficult to come out early if the hive had faced west, I thought, standing on the alighting board which was still damp with dew, wiping my eyes and antennae. I flew off to the poppies again, resolved to bring back as much pollen as I could. To my surprise, many of the flowers on which I had worked the day before were already losing their petals. Others, however, were

". . . climbing roses. Their large, white, single flowers, open to the evening sky, stood out clearly in the slowly descending dusk."

newly opening in their place, the pollen abundant and invitingly fresh.

I continued my work, seeing within my field of vision several other bees who were equally busy, but I did not know whether they came from our hive or from either of the other two. The rule was, I knew, that foragers never waste time in talking, even less in quarrelling over the crop. The right time to talk is inside the hive, when feeding each other, co-operating in housework, or when resting in the cluster. During foraging, no co-operation is possible. "Each bee depends only on herself, and answers for what she carries into the hive". I must have been told this part of the Hive Legend long ago, and now it surfaced in my memory, as always, at the appropriate time.

I had already returned with several loads of pollen; and, feeling that I was entitled to take a rest, stopped on the comb to clean myself. Then I went up to the honey storage area, found an empty cell, crawled in, and for a time became oblivious to what was taking place around me. However, after some time, the activity became so feverish that it could no longer be ignored, and I backed out of my temporary quarters.

A few nectar gatherers were in the middle of a furious dance. There was obviously very important news. Their enthusiasm was infectious, and I began to follow one of the dancers. She gave me a drop of nectar: it was very good nectar, although not exceptionally strong, with a slightly minty flavour, but not nearly as pronounced as it would be in mint. What the dance indicated, however, was abundance. It was a round, figure-of-eight dance, performed at high speed. The nectar was very close, but where? Anyway, I already had a crop which I was working. Should I abandon my poppies for the sake of nectar?

The dancers were so insistent that I went out to look for the source. The dance could not have referred to any garden flowers, as no one variety predominated to such an extent. Trees, then? I circled higher, and very soon noticed that bees were flying to the end of the garden, to the lime trees, which were such a familiar feature just over the fence. I took a closer look. All the limes were now covered with small, hanging clusters of buds; and here and there, one of the buds was already opening into a greenish flower. It was another upside-down flower, like borage, only smaller. One had to suspend

oneself from it, feet up, to reach the centre. I did this, and found that nectar was oozing out between the sepals. It was very easy to collect, and I moved quickly from flower to flower.

The bunches were invitingly near to each other. At one point, however, I became aware that the pattern of branches had changed. I looked round, and saw that, moving constantly in the same south-easterly direction, I was now on a neighbouring tree. This one had an even greater proportion of flowers opened, and they were almost dripping with nectar. It was not possible to go away and do something else, leaving all those riches behind. I remembered the Hive Legend: "During a good nectar flow, leave everything that can be left, apart from the brood. All other work can wait, but a flow might last only a short time."

This rule would apply to my pollen, of course. It would have to wait for me, or for another bee, to go back to it as time permitted. We had to make sure not only that there would be enough food to rear our future babies and for day-to-day use, but also to keep in mind the needs of the colony in winter. As the Hive Legend tells: "A colony can never have too much put aside for the winter."

I remembered that when I had first heard about winter, when it may not be possible to leave the hive for many weeks at a time and when there are no flowers, I had found it quite impossible to imagine. Now, having lived through a few days when we were confined to the hive and all our stores ran out, I found it a little easier. Bees must be provided with stores for the winter, however hard the work of collecting them might be. I was lucky to be a summer bee. Those who were destined to live through the winter could only do so if we, the summer bees, provided for them.

As I worked on the lime blossom, I discovered that I would still be able to supply pollen to feed the brood, with only a little extra effort. Lime pollen

Evaporating the nectar

was being dislodged from the flowers and showered on to my body without any specific effort to gather it. I could hang by one front leg, brush it off and pack my baskets without expending too much energy in trying to hover with a full honey sac. This I did, again and again.

The resulting load – nectar in my honey stomach and pollen in my baskets – was heavy, but there was no need to fly far.

The lime tree on which I was working was gradually becoming crowded with bees: not only my sisters, the honeybees, but also bumble-bees, some huge and hairy, others smaller, about the same size as ourselves, but also covered with thick fur. There were even flies. The tree was providing more than enough for all, and certainly much more than we could ever hope to gather by ourselves. We went out again and again, bringing in the nectar, passing it to the housebees in the hive, and unpacking our small, but constantly renewed loads of pollen into the cells.

All the forager bees were now at work. Only the nurses who looked after the Queen and the bees who were processing our nectar stayed inside. It was perhaps a good thing that as yet we had no brood to care for: all our energies could be concentrated on the lime flow. Even so, more nectar was coming in than could possibly be evaporated at once, and a huge backlog was now building up.

In the late afternoon, as I was giving up a load, there was a quick exchange between myself and a receiving bee.

"We can't keep it up" she said. "We'll have to work at night to evaporate all this."

"We are all going to work at night, taking turns" I answered, and flew out once more.

I allowed myself a short rest before joining the others in the nectar evaporation. About a hundred of us formed a chain and began to drive the air, saturated with moisture, out of the hive exit. It was quite dark by now, as I saw when I had finished my turn at fanning and took a peep outside. There was no time at this stage to loiter on the balcony. Those who were not busy actually dispelling the moisture-laden air were needed inside the hive to raise the temperature in order to speed up evaporation. We snatched short resting periods between one activity and another, but there was no quiet corner in the hive in which anyone could be left in peace for long, except perhaps the empty comb in which nectar had not yet been placed, above the main work area. Most of the combs, however, already contained cells which were at least partly filled.

The Queen lays her first eggs

By the time the activity became less intense, it was well past midnight. As the air cooled before dawn, we clustered for a short while, talking together and preparing for a new day. When it came, we were impatient to begin work and could hardly wait for the early morning greyness to give way to the sun before we were back at the lime trees. When I went out for the first time, it was still cool, but the flowers were almost dripping with nectar.

Returning to the hive, I roused my sisters with the most energetic round dance of which I was capable. I was soon followed by more dancers with the same message. "Nectar is there for the taking. Come out and get it!"

The pattern of work was similar to that of the previous day. Concentrating on the side of the tree which faced the sun, where nectar flowed more generously, we filled up to capacity, brushed any accidentally-collected pollen into our baskets, and took both crops to the hive. House bees, again, could not quite cope with the work, and a lot of our nectar was temporarily spread on the inside walls of the cells to dry a little before it could be processed properly. From time to time, we took short rests in the hive, and then went out to forage once more.

When at last evening came and I returned for the night, exhausted, there was subdued excitement due, I suspected, to something more than the prodigious amount of nectar which had been collected. The housebees had news for us: on one of the combs, right in the centre, the Queen had laid a few eggs. They were her first, of course, and she was still inexperienced, so that occasionally two, or even three appeared in one cell, and the surplus had to be removed by the nurses. But we did not worry, knowing from the Hive Legend that this would soon pass as the Queen learned the technique. She was now being fed and groomed by the younger bees with special care, and Queen substance was being passed round to all of us, as if in celebration of this important day in our colony's history.

Threatening weather

Next day the heat increased, and in the afternoon it became oppressive. Clouds began to gather in the south and raced diagonally across the sky, becoming darker and darker as they came, and finally appearing almost navy-blue. I was half-way through a session of work on the limes when I noticed the change of light. Then came a flash of lightning, still distant, so that the thunder that followed was almost like an afterthought and appeared to be disconnected from the flash. I had never witnessed a thunderstorm when outside the hive, but felt curiously unworried by it. Home was very close. There was time enough to return to it, and perhaps the storm might even pass us by.

I continued to work, trying to hurry, just in case the rain came and forced me to stop soon. Catching sight of other bees nearby, I saw that some were leaving to go home, but perhaps that was only because their honey stomachs were already full. I decided to trust my inner voice and stay.

The huge cloud moved slowly from the south towards the east, but taking a circular route and not coming any nearer, almost as if by-passing our garden. It finally disappeared into the distance. The sun, slowly nearing the west, bathed everything around us with brilliance.

I was glad of my decision to stay until my work was finished.

In the evening, I talked it over with my sisters. It appeared that very few had been frightened into returning.

"There is something about this in the Hive Legend" said one of the oldest bees. "When a storm might be coming, do not trust your eyes. Trust the way you feel."

I did not remember being told this before, but the advice was sound. We had all been very upset by the previous storm, which heralded the long rain, even though we were inside the hive. Seeing the cloud today had not given us the same feeling at all.

There was a certain monotony in the days that followed. The weather was again settled, and all the lime trees behind the fence burst into bloom. We had time only for the effort to secure this bonanza for the future. I would have lost all count of time, were it not for the fact that its passing could now be measured by the growth of our new generation.

A new brood is hatched

The first eggs of our Queen hatched after three days. We, the nectar gatherers, were told the news on our return to the hive. There was a patch of cells, about six bee-lengths across, the result of the Queen's first day of laying, which now contained not eggs, but tiny grubs, each one floating on top of a little pool of food. We were given a progress report each day; and, as we had all been nurses at one time, we knew exactly, without having to touch the babies, what they were like. They grew into fat larvae, and we followed their development closely, although we were not directly involved in their care.

Our nights were spent partly in evaporating the nectar gathered during the day, and partly in talking together. I was now one of the senior bees in the colony, and had to make sure that the younger generation would know all about the Hive Legend. We spoke of winter, of the necessarily frugal existence which does not allow bees to keep their drones, and of our enemies. Because we had gone out with a cast, there were no bees in the colony that were really young and inexperienced. They all knew at first hand about swarming, about hunger, and the mating of Queens. All the same, they had to be reminded to pass on the Legend so that, when bees of my age were no longer there and the present day nurses became foragers, they would be able to bridge the month-long generation gap between themselves and the daughters of our Queen.

These new bees would have to learn quickly, as they were destined to be in charge of the hive at a younger age than would normally be expected.

It was now fifteen days since we had left the old hive. Our cast, which had experienced such a difficult start because of the long spell of rain, was now a colony with brood, but we still had to wait for quite a while before the first bees would be born to augment our numbers.

The most violent storm of my life

Two days later, we were told that our eldest larvae had been sealed in their cells. It would be twelve days before they were ready to come out as adult bees. Around the area of sealed cells was a ring of open brood, spiralling outwards into smaller and smaller larvae, the outer edge of the circle containing eggs. The Queen had learned very quickly how to lay one egg to a cell, and the brood comb was now beautifully even. This was the comb I had helped to build, I thought with pride.

Our work on the lime flowers, meanwhile, followed the same daily routine. Not knowing how long the nectar flow would last, we were taking no risks by slowing down our tempo of work. Our storage combs now contained more and more fully-ripened and sealed honey.

There came a time, however, when we recognised the fact that the flow would soon end. We all worked hard that day. It was very hot and close; and the monotony of working on the lime flowers was soothing. Earlier, there had been no need to search for the flowers, as they were all around; but lately I had noticed that most of them were already faded, and I had to look into the distance occasionally, breaking the rhythm of activity and seeking flowers which were still young.

Suddenly I felt, rather than saw, a disturbance, and stopped. I looked at the sky. It was rapidly becoming darker. What drew my attention even more than the change of light was a stream of bees swooping down from the trees at the end of the garden towards the hives. There was no hesitation whatever in that rush to get away from the storm, not this time. I left my flower and joined the others. Close to the hives, we divided into three streams. Mine was the one on the left. I landed and ran in, gratefully, just as the first heavy drops of rain began to fall. Some of my sisters who staggered after me were already drenched, heavy with water, their feet sticking to the floor. They needed a moment or so to rest before they could wipe the water off their faces and bodies, and sometimes they left a small puddle where previously they had been standing.

Rain thundered against the hive roof. It was the most violent storm of my life, but fortunately quite brief. Long before sunset, it ceased, and a brightness outside indicated that the sun had come out. There was now so much light

"I stayed on the hand a little longer, enjoying the comfort, and then began to walk up the finger to find a good take-off position."

Reflections prove disorientating

that I felt it was safe to fly out again. That, I would soon learn, was quite a rash decision.

The alighting board was dripping wet. I took off carefully, flew up above the hive, and looked around. The garden was again somewhat unfamiliar, as if something had basically changed since I had taken all those careful observation flights. The sun and the sky were now reflected in large pools of water, where before there had been only grass. The hives were slightly raised; but around them the ground dipped in several places, and in those places water had collected. The sun shimmered on all the watery surfaces. Orientation was difficult. Even the roof of the hive seemed to disappear, and in its place I saw only a subdued reflection of the sky. The world seemed to have no top and no bottom, and I found it difficult to judge height.

I flew towards the lime trees, a little uncertainly, but was disappointed. Water still dripped thickly from the leaves and branches, and no bee in her senses would risk going under that stream. Anyway, all the nectar had probably been washed away. I circled, trying to regain my bearings and to familiarize myself with the unexpectedly new situation. There seemed nothing that I could usefully do outside so I decided to go home.

I was already directly over the hive roof, when a huge drop of water, detached from the overhanging branches, hit my whole body, and knocked me down. I landed on the roof. Blinded and shaken, I

A smaller, human hand

tried to regain my balance, but instead, dragged down by the weight of the water, I found myself on my back. I attempted to turn over, to stand on my feet, but something was holding me down. My legs were in the air; and as I moved them, there was no resistance, nothing within reach I could use to pull myself up from this helpless position. My eyes were under water, and I could see practically nothing. I was firmly stuck to the wet roof surface. A chill came up from the water in which I lay, taking over my whole body. Trying to conserve my remains of energy, I folded my legs together and lay quietly. There was nothing that I could do. If I had not made the mistake of going out immediately after the rain, I would have been of use to the colony for a little longer, perhaps until the young bees were born. It was now too late to do anything about it.

I do not know how long I lay on my back in the water, but for the second time in my life something quite unaccountable happened. Something pulled me by my feet. It was quite uncomfortable, as the drag of the water on my wings was very strong, but they were finally released. I was put on a warm and resilient surface. It reminded me of the time when the bee-keeper had allowed me to walk to the end of his finger to fly. Now I could not fly. I was too cold; but I recognized that the thing on which I stood was again a human hand.

It curved round my body, radiating warmth. Life was slowly returning, and I began to pulsate my abdomen in breathing movements. Hesitatingly, I raised my front legs to wipe water from my head and antennae, and as normal feeling was gradually restored, I dried each part of my body in turn. I touched the hand in which I was enclosed with my antennae. I did not know who had saved me, and we had no way of communicating; but I could feel a wave of sympathy directed towards me, and I tried to convey the same in return.

The hand opened slightly. The flight muscles in my thorax vibrated, became warmer, and tuned to the pitch needed for flying. I stayed on the hand a little longer, enjoying the comfort, and then began to walk up the finger to find a good take-off position. It was then that I noticed that the finger was much smaller than the one belonging to the bee-keeper. Was this

Important work to complete before winter

a smaller bee-keeper perhaps, and would it grow bigger, the way our larvae were at first small and then grew? It seemed unlikely. Larvae grow because they are only babies, and bees do not grow once they have attained their adult shape. But this hand was the same shape as that of the bee-keeper, and therefore it could not be a baby. This was something I could not quite understand.

I reached the top, wiped my antennae twice more, raised my front legs off the finger tip and flew away. It was high time. The sun was just setting, and it was already cold. I entered the hive, pushed in among my sisters, feeling their presence all round me, and asked for food, which was at once given. The warmth and companionship had never been more welcome than that evening.

When I walked out on to the alighting board the next morning, it was cool and fresh after the previous day's rain. The pools of water which had formed around the garden were almost gone, but I felt in no hurry to fly out, and waited for the sun to warm up the world a little before starting work. I wandered about the hive, but had not worked inside for a long time, and found that there was not much which I felt like doing. One thing struck me, though, during the walkabout, and that was the very small amount of propolis now used in the structure of our home. In an old hive, there was always a lot of propolis, which could be taken out of one place and re-used in another according to need. But ours was now a new hive; and having so many other pressing duties, we had not yet seen to it that all the cracks were filled and ends of frames made secure.

"Because bees nest in hollow trees, sometimes very high up, they must guard against wind. There must be no cracks through which a draught can blow in winter. The only opening to be left is the one used by the bees," said the Hive Legend.

We did not live in a hollow tree high up, but the Hive Legend was quite definite on the subject, and had to be followed faithfully. It would be very important to have this work completed before winter, I thought.

A few of the foraging bees had left, and I was just proposing to do the same, when they returned. The limes by the fence had abruptly ceased to produce nectar; the last of it had been washed out by the previous day's downpour. We would have to look for another source. There was still room to store more nectar, to make sure that the winter bees would survive until spring. We wanted to fill every available cell with honey.

A new source of nectar

Scouts were sent out farther afield. They soon returned bringing back good news, so good that I could hardly believe it. Their furious dance showed us that there was a new source of nectar, straight towards the west, at a little over two hundred yards. But the most amazing part of the message was that the nectar was also lime, and not only lime, but a much sweeter, better sort of lime. How was this possible?

The source was easy to find. Beyond the large patch of grass in which wild flowers grew there were a few trees. They were smaller than our limes. Their leaves were also smaller and darker green, but at the moment they were almost invisible under a mass of pale, creamy yellow bracts, enclosing bunches of buds, some of which were just opening into the familiar, though smaller lime blossoms. Once they were all fully-opened, their numbers would be prodigious.

I joined the other bees on the very top of the tree, where more flowers were open than lower down, and set to work. The scent of the blossom in the full sun, but in the still damp atmosphere, was almost enough to make one dizzy.

The foraging continues

I worked on the small-leaved limes for several days. Not all the trees came into flower at once; and on each of them the flowers opened in sequence, beginning near the top on the sunny side of the tree, and gradually spreading to lower branches. Even within one cluster, some had opened, flowered and faded before others were ready. In this way, there was always nectar available somewhere for every bee who went to collect it.

Our house bees were now beginning to have difficulty in finding storage space for all that was being brought in, especially the temporary space needed for the nectar before evaporation, which took up much more room than ripened honey. In order to accommodate it, additional comb had to be made wherever there was any space in the hive. It now took us longer to dispose of our load before flying out again, and for this reason we were less inclined to hurry when foraging.

On one occasion, instead of going straight to the limes, I began to examine other trees in the neighbourhood, although they were not in flower. At the back of my mind there was still the need to search for propolis, which would have to be taken seriously sooner or later. One tree in particular interested me. It had no flowers at all, and no leaves either. The twigs were covered instead by bunches of long, thin spikes; and in many places tiny droplets of sticky resin oozed out of the bark.

I circled the trunk to alight on the sunny side, found the sticky substance and began to tug at it with my mandibles. Being warm, it started to stretch in a thread. I lifted my head and pulled hard. The elongated thread snapped at last. I had to roll it up, moistening my legs and mandibles with saliva, so as not to become hopelessly entangled. I succeeded in forming the thread into a little ball and placed it in one of my pollen baskets. A lot of work was needed before I had collected a reasonable load in this way. It was not nearly as large as a pollen load would have been, but at least as heavy. But there was one worry which I did not have: that it might fall out of the baskets. The opposite was the case.

On returning home, I was forced to sit on an outside wall of the hive, in the sun, so that my harvest would again become soft enough to be removed. Even then, I was unable to do this myself, and had to go inside and ask some house bees for assistance. They were busy receiving nectar, but two of them agreed to unload my propolis for me. By scraping and pulling in different directions, they at last emptied my baskets. One bee then went back to her nectar. The other stayed behind, and helped me to make a start at filling a gap between the crownboard and one of the walls of the hive. Small amounts of the resinous propolis had to be moulded with our mandibles, and pushed into the gap as far as we could reach.

When all the material I had gathered was used up, I felt a great sense of achievement. But I knew, of course, that many more trips by many bees would be needed before the whole hive would be completely weatherproofed.

"I am not going to be here much longer" I told the younger bee, as we rested together. "Anyway, it is still rather too early in the season to gather propolis; it is not normally done during a honeyflow. But please remember to carry on the work before the cold weather comes."

"I will, Deborah; and I will pass it on to the autumn bees" she promised.

The autumn bees, I thought. Even the bees who were soon to be born would no longer be here when autumn came. They were summer bees, like myself, although they would probably live until late in the season. We all had to pass on the Hive Legend so that, although individual bees did not live long, there would be no break in the life of the family. Each generation could only contribute according to the time of year in which it lived, but at the same time had to know about the whole hive year in order to pass the whole Legend on.

The future colony is assured

At last the time came for our Queen's daughters to be born. I met one of the youngsters straight out of her cell, still unsure on her legs, and offered her fresh lime nectar. I also shared with her my name, as she would soon be taking my place in the hive.

"Welcome to the family, Deborah" I said, as she accepted the food, her first as an adult bee.

We were all happy to greet the newcomers. Our future as a colony was assured. We had won through.

For me, life had turned full circle. After a few days, as more and more bees were born, I felt that I had contributed as much as I was able and I was tired. That afternoon, I made a trip to the lime trees, and then returned to the garden: but instead of going into the hive, I alighted on a leaf and stayed there. My mind went back to the old bee I had met as a youngster as she was dying in front of the hive, happy that her family was strong and would soon send out a swarm. We had worked hard. We had sent out two swarms. Now I knew with certainty that the families in the three hives which stood side by side all came from the same stock.

Slowly, the afternoon turned into evening. The last of my sisters were flying home, but I no longer felt the urge to join them. I sat looking at the garden which was bathed in the last rays of the setting sun, not hurrying any more. The last stragglers went back into the hive, just in time to escape the chill that always descends after sunset. I remained, enjoying the evening as long as the light lasted. For the first time, I was happy to be alone. But perhaps I was not really alone. In spirit, I was with my sisters in the hive. I would always be part of it.

Deborah was born on 31st May.

She died on 15th July, having lived the full life-span of a summer bee.

NOTES

ABDOMEN This is the rear part of the bee's body. It contains the digestive system and the honey stomach or honey sac, into which nectar is collected.

ALIGHTING or LANDING BOARD. This is a strip of wood attached in front of the entrance of some types of hive. Bees usually pause on it before going in and out of the hive. A great deal of bee activity is easily observed on the alighting board. Young bees seek out the darkest parts of the hive; and only as they become older, do they spend more time in or near the lighter areas or on the alighting board.

ANTENNAE These are the jointed feelers found on the head of bees, as well as various other insects. Latest research suggests that when their antennae touch, bees lock into one other's nervous systems. If so, then communication between them is probably instant and complete. All the 'conversations' between bees in this story are based on this theory.

BASKETS Worker honey-bees have on each of their back legs a hollow structure surrounded by hairs, in which pollen is collected and brought back to the hive. These are called *corbicula* or, more commonly, pollen baskets.

BORAGE *Borago officinalis* or *Bee borage* is a cottage-garden plant, long in favour with bees and bee-keepers. It gives a steady flow of nectar with a high concentration of sugar.

BROOD The term is used collectively and refers to bees in the early stages of development – that is, eggs, larvae, and pupae.

CAPPED CELLS When nectar has been fully evaporated and turned into honey, the cells where it lies are capped or sealed with a wax lid. Honey is hygroscopic: that is, it attracts moisture from the air. If left exposed, it would again become diluted and be in danger of fermenting.

CASTS Further swarms, which issue occasionally after the prime swarm, headed by the old Queen, has already left, are known as *casts*. They are headed by unmated, virgin Queens and are usually smaller than the main swarm. *See also* Queen Cells.

COMBS Providing the 'furniture' of the hive, comb is used for brood-rearing and storage according to need and the time of year. Bees build comb initially of wax, but other substances are incorporated later with use. Individual combs hang vertically, parallel to one another, with space for bees to move between them. Each comb consists of hexagonal cells, arranged back to back on either side of the common mid-rib. The cells are of two sizes: smaller cells in which worker brood is reared, and larger ones for drone brood. Either size can be used for storing honey. They are tilted slightly upwards so that the contents will remain in place.

A comb-building cluster of bees normally anchors itself at the top, and the comb is built downwards by the hanging bees. *See also* Honey Cells.

COTONEASTER There are many shrubs in this group, and all are visited by bees. *C. horizontalis*, sometimes called *Herringbone cotoneaster* on account of its shape is a favourite bee plant.

CROWNBOARD This is the bee-keeping term for the board placed on top of the hive box, under the roof. From the bee's point-of-view, it would be seen as a ceiling.

DANCES Forager bees inform other members of the colony about the location of forage by means of dancing. Karl von Frisch, who discovered the dance language of bees, describes two kinds of dance: a *round* dance, used when the forage is less than twenty-five yards from the hive, and which does not specify the direction; and a *wagtail dance*, when forage is at a greater distance. Directional information in the horizontal plane is expressed as the angle from the sun. The bee, running on the vertical comb, translates the information into the vertical plane, the upward run indicating the direction of the sun, and the angle from the vertical expressing the angle from the sun. The bee indicates the distance at which forage is to be found by the speed of the run and of the final 'wag'. The greater the distance, the more slowly the dance is performed. Similar dances are performed on the surface of the swarm cluster by scouts looking for a new home, when they have found a possible site for the colony.

DRONES The fact that drones, (male bees) are produced from unfertilized eggs was first observed by Dzierzon in 1845. It is now known that the rule applies to most insects of the order *Hymenoptera*, as well as to honeybees. Although they are larger than workers, and buzz more loudly, drones have no sting. A drone's main task is to fertilize a young Queen, after which he dies. Drones doubtless play other roles in the complex society of the hive, but these are not yet fully understood. When bees build their own comb, they may produce large quantities of drone brood, as much as fifteen to twenty per cent at the height of the season. By supplying them with worker foundation, bee-keepers may reduce that number to a few hundred per hive, but any repairs to comb by the bees are likely to contain drone cells in which more drones are reared. Drones are usually present in the colony from about April to late summer.

FORAGERS These are bees who leave the hive to forage outside, and gather mainly pollen and nectar. They are also known as *field bees*.

HONEY CELLS Ordinarily, brood occupies the centre of each comb, and a ring of cells containing pollen surrounds the brood. Honey is stored outside of this ring of pollen cells. The whole effect is that of a hard-boiled egg, sliced in half: the yolk is the brood; the white, the pollen; and the shell, honey. Notably, there is a tendency to store most of the honey above the brood. Thus, Deborah finally reaches the honey storage area by climbing up from the brood.

HONEY SAC This part of the honey-bee's stomach into which nectar is collected is divided from the stomach proper by a valve. When full, it occupies nearly a third of the abdomen.

HONEYFLOW Although, strictly speaking, the term 'nectar flow' would be a more correct one to use, this is how bee-keepers refer to the period during which one or more types of plant secrete enough nectar for bees to collect and store large quantities. The duration of a honeyflow depends, of course, on the plant, its location and the weather.

HOUSE BEES In the first three weeks of their lives, bees work mainly inside the hive. As house-bees, their duties progress from cleaning to the nursing of larvae, and then to receiving nectar from incoming foragers, to wax secretion and to comb-building.

LARVA This is the bee at an early stage of development, after it has hatched from the egg.

MANDIBLES These are the paired jaws of the bee.

NECTAR A sugar solution produced by plants, when nectar has been collected by bees, it is turned into honey as a result of partial evaporation and enzyme activity.

NURSES Bees work as nurses when they are between three and twelve days old, their glands producing a secretion with which larvae are fed. As these glands develop, the nurses begin to feed older larvae; and at their peak, they feed young brood or Queen larvae. Once their glands begin to atrophy, bees go back to feeding older brood.

PROBOSCIS This is the bee's tongue, comprising several parts which together form a hollow sucking tube.

QUEEN CELLS Bees intending to swarm usually make many more Queen cells than needed. One is necessary to take over the colony: others, if allowed to remain, would head further swarms or *casts*, each taking with it about half of the bees present in the hive at the time. This might eventually threaten the colony's survival by weakening it too much. Bees often prevent this themselves, by destroying superfluous Queens. Otherwise, the duty to remove them falls to the bee-keeper, in whose interest it is to keep the colony strong. This is one of the basic tasks of colony management.

QUEEN SUBSTANCE This complex organic acid, secreted by glands found in the Queen's head, is distributed by bees after they have groomed and fed the Queen. Its presence in turn confirms the presence of the Queen, prevents the development of the workers' ovaries, and consolidates the colony as a social unit. When there is not enough of the Queen substance in the colony, workers begin to rear new Queens in preparation for either swarming or replacement.

ROBINIA Commonly known as *Acacia*, this tree is native to the eastern USA, where it is also known as the *Locust tree*. It has been widely cultivated in Europe, and is a valuable honey plant in Hungary. In Britain, it fills the gap between the spring and summer flowering trees, when there is not much bee forage. Acacia honey does not crystalize easily, and remains in a liquid state for a long time.

ROYAL JELLY This is bee milk, or brood food, that is fed to Queen larvae. There are certain chemical differences between the food given to worker and Queen larvae, although both are glandular secretions.

SEPALS These are outer floral leaves.

TASTE-SMELL In bees, these two senses are much more closely related than in humans, and it is thought that the bee probably tastes and smells with the same organs, known as *pit-pegs*, which are situated on the antennae.

THORAX This is the middle part of the bee's body, to which the wings and legs are attached. It also contains the flight muscles.

VISION Bee vision extends more closely to the ultra-violet end of the spectrum than our own. Bees therefore see ultra-violet and notice patterns on certain flowers which to us remain invisible. They see blue especially well, because of its proximity to violet. What is more, it is one of their favourite colours. However, they do not see red, which to them appears black. Red poppies are an exception, because they reflect ultra-violet light.

Each of the bee's compound eyes comprises about 6,900 lenses, and is well adapted to detecting movement. The bee's measure of sensitivity to flicker is about 300 per second, compared with 30 per second in humans: so that a bee looking at a film would see it as a series of separate pictures. A film projected for bees would therefore have to run ten times faster before the images fused into continual movement.

FURTHER READING

Brown, R. BEE-KEEPING: A SEASONAL GUIDE. Batsford, 1985.

Butler, C.G. THE WORLD OF THE HONEYBEE. Collins, 1974.

Free, J.B. THE SOCIAL ORGANISATION OF HONEYBEES. Edward Arnold, 1977.

Frisch, Karl von. THE DANCING BEES. Methuen, 1966. (Account of the discovery and study of the bees' dance communication, and much more.)

Hodges, D. POLLEN LOADS OF THE HONEYBEE, I.B.R.A., 1975. (The variety of shape and colour of various pollens comes to life in this book by an artist-beekeeper.)

Hooper, Ted. GUIDE TO BEES AND HONEY. Blandford Press, 1976. (Introduction to bees and bee-keeping.)

Powell, John. THE WORLD OF A BEEHIVE. Faber & Faber, 1979. (Introduction to honeybees, written with the young student in mind.)